The Martyrs of Guanabara

The Martyrs of Guanabara

John Gillies

MOODY PRESS
CHICAGO

For Carolyn

© 1976 by
THE MOODY BIBLE INSTITUTE
OF CHICAGO

Library of Congress Cataloging in Publication Data

Gillies, John, 1925-
 The martyrs of Guanabara.

 1. La Fon, André—Fiction. 2. Villegaignon,
Nicholas Durand de, 1510-1571?—Fiction. I. Title.
PZ4.G48187Mar [PS3557.1387] 813'.5'4 76-14954
ISBN 0-8024-5187-X

Printed in the United States of America

Contents

Foreword

During the century before Englishmen first arrived in Jamestown and Plymouth, people of three nations were busily exploring and establishing their empires in South America. Those nations were Spain, Portugal, and France.

This story is about the French experience, at a site which today is the sprawling megalopolis of Rio de Janeiro.

The story is also about the French Reformation, whose songs and prayers were among the very first to be raised in praise and petition in the Western Hemisphere.

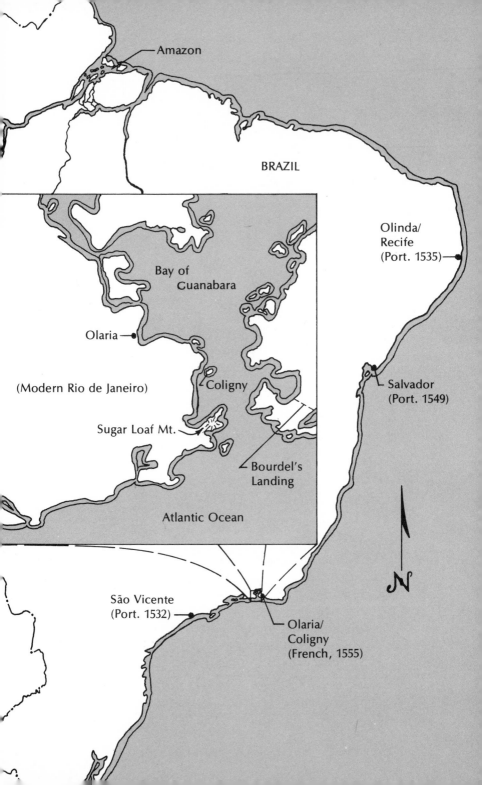

1. La Fon

In the fading twilight, I stumbled and fell, with a cry of pain.

"André, are you all right?" someone shouted. My four companions had been walking ahead of me, but they must have heard my fall and shout because they ran back to where I had fallen in the underbrush.

"I only tripped over this stupid root of a tree," I said. "And I knocked off my glasses!"

"Let's hope they're not broken!" said Jean du Bourdel.

I shouldn't have been wearing them. Usually I wear glasses only when I am tailoring, but I have a difficult enough time seeing, and in this strange darkness of the forest I could hardly make my way. As I groped for my glasses, I felt something leathery and cold. And with a scream I perceived it was a human hand.

Pierre Bourdon raised me to my feet, handing me my glasses which he had seen in the brush.

"You tripped over a body, not a root of a tree!" said Bourdel. Jean was our leader in this unhappy adventure. Even in the dim light we saw the outlines of a body, lying face downward. Bourdel reached down and turned the body over.

"Well, he's a European," said Pierre with a sigh.

"I wonder who he is," muttered Bourdel.

"That is Carmeau!" Matthieu Verneuil asserted. I said I could not believe it. "That is Carmeau!" Matthieu insisted. "One of the old colonists. One of our old comrades."

"How could anyone be certain of who he is?" snapped Pierre.

In a way, I agreed. The body was shriveled and quite beyond recognition. And it was dark, and we could not see clearly. Also I was becoming conscious of the sickening sweet smell of decayed flesh.

"I know it is Carmeau," Matthieu declared. "I worked with the man on the island. I was there the day the admiral sent him away."

"I'm sorry," said Pierre, shaking his head in a kind of apology.

"Damn Villegaignon!"

The four of us stared at Jacques le Balleur. Such a strange man he was. For the most part he kept to himself and kept his silence. But he could burst into flame like a field of dry grass, without warning. His anger, when it erupted, continued to surprise me.

9

"There's no need to curse," said Bourdel. "Not even the admiral."

"After all that he's done?" Jacques turned his head and spat. "Bourdel, this poor peasant here probably starved to death. Look at him! Look at us! He's dead and we're dying. As is the colony of New France. And our church. And the cause of it all is that fat boar!"

"But we must not curse any man," Bourdel repeated quietly.

"I pray to God that He will never grant peace to Admiral Villegaignon." Jacques glared at Bourdel. "For me, Bourdel, it is petition, a prayer to Almighty God: God damn Villegaignon!"

"But may He grant peace to this poor soul," said Bourdel calmly, "whether he be Carmeau or whoever he might be. And he should be buried."

"I tell you, he's Carmeau!" again declared Matthieu.

"So be it," said Bourdel. "Before we heard your shout, André," he looked at me, "we thought we heard the lapping waves of water ahead. If so, it would be easier to bury our friend in the sand."

We walked more slowly, carrying our burden, forced to be more cautious because of the darkness. Soon I began to hear the lapping waves, and within ten minutes we saw the water.

The five of us began digging a hole in the sand, scooping it out with our hands, as we had no tools. Pierre and Matthieu lowered the body into the sandy grave.

Jean du Bourdel remained on his knees.

" 'I am the resurrection and the life!' says the Lord. 'He who believes in me shall never die.' "

We added our amens.

" 'Absent from the body, present with the Lord!' " Jean then led us in praying the prayer our Lord had taught his disciples.

We moved closer to shore and sat quietly, staring across the water.

"Do you realize where God has led us?" Bourdel asked suddenly. "Look! It is our bay!"

It was true. The moon was rising and a soft faint glow improved our vision. It is a beautiful bay, this body of water the Portuguese, in their ignorance, had called a river. The Rio de Janeiro, the River of January! We could now clearly see the curved stone mountains to our left, towards the entrance to the bay.

Behind us was a forest we had traversed for a day and a half. Beyond that forest, toward the east where the sun had set, was another beach where we had left our sickly craft. And beyond that shore was the great ocean upon which our friends, our loved ones, the members of our Christian fellowship were sailing. To think that we had been with them only a week ago, that together we thought we had finally escaped the horrors caused by a demented tyrant!

Home and sanity in France now seemed so far away.

Ahead of us, across this beautiful bay, was Coligny, the colony of French Antartica, as our governor had named this part of Brazil. The governor was the admiral whom we both feared and hated: Nicholas Durand de Villegaignon.

"André, look!" Matthieu broke my reverie and handed me a cluster of bananas. "There are many of them here!"

"I wonder if Carmeau knew they were here," I said.

I suppose a person could starve to death if all he had to eat were bananas. These were filling—as bananas always are for me—and I became drowsy. It had been a long day of marching, and now that hunger was assuaged, weariness took over.

Before falling asleep, I remember wondering when I, André La Fon, a fairly good tailor from Le Havre, would ever again see my homeland.

2. Villegaignon

Nicholas Durand de Villegaignon stood before the mirror in his personal quarters on the island fortress of Coligny. He was pleased with what he saw, preening himself with comb and brush, posing this way and that. He was a nobleman, a vice admiral, and a Frenchman! Some were saying he was putting on too much weight; but as he felt his rotund stomach, he decided his girth was proper and befitting for a person of his rank and responsibility. Yes, he was enormously pleased with what he saw in his mirror.

But then the admiral frowned. That enlarging girth of his was presenting problems for his wardrobe. He had ten uniforms, and all were now in need of alteration. And he would like to have a new uniform or two. He would have them if André La Fon, the only tailor of the colony, had not left with those bloody Huguenots.

Bloody Huguenots! It was a good characterization. He had learned the term from his Scots guards, who probably learned it from some English prisoners. Perhaps he was more bloody than they, in more literal and even vulgar terms. But Huguenots were the most sanguine people he had ever known. Enthusiastic, energetic, hopeful—and fanatical!

But he would force himself not to think about those accursed Huguenots today. They had affected his state of mind for too long. They were gone—at least most of them were gone. He had heard that two or three Huguenots still remained in Olaria, on the mainland. However, his personal tribulation with these Reformers had ended when that last group set sail on that miserable bark, the *Jacques.* They had been gone for some two weeks now! And it was good riddance. He would put them out of his mind. It was only a matter of will, and the admiral was a firm believer in the strength of his will.

He decided to wear his dark blue trousers and a white tunic. It was January—equivalent to July in France—and it would be a very warm day. He fondled the fresh, starched whiteness of his tunic. How very fortunate he was!

"Tupí!" he shouted.

She quickly appeared. He was certain she had been waiting for his call.

"Bon jour, mon admiral!" she smiled. Her French was improving.

"Good morning, mon cheri!" he beamed in reply. "I am ready for my breakfast."

She seemed to dance out of the room.

Tupí was the name of an Indian tribe, and the admiral fancied its sound. And his Tupí was surely a great gift and a delight. In this strange, hostile world this savage was his. Much more than a slave: a maid, a cook, an ironer of his tunics—and a mistress. Why not admit it? Besides, who would know in France?

And who would care, in France?

To be sure, he had forbidden any socializing with the savages, particularly with Indian women. That had not made him more popular with his men; but, of course, it was a necessary restriction.

As for himself, he had been cautious. As the leader of this colony, he made the laws. He could live by them or he could modify them—as he deemed best! Here on this French outpost in the New World, on this island named for Gaspard Coligny, chief of the French admiralty, he, Nicholas Villegaignon, was king. The thought of being king amused him. Nicholas the first! What a remarkable king he would make in some place where being a king had more meaning than here. Somewhat guiltily he frowned and paid his mental respects to his sovereign lord, King Henry II.

Tupí returned with a freshly cut papaya, some fresh bread, fruit marmalade, and coffee. He waved her away with a gesture of thanks and a smile. He liked to savor this early moment of the day alone. There would be time to spend with Tupí later in the day. After all, he, the admiral, was a man of discipline.

He drank his coffee slowly. It was a pity the cow had died. Café au lait would be delicious. And butter for the hot bread!

But there was still coffee, his one last luxury in these deplorable days. The beans were getting a bit rancid, and he had ordered a new supply. However, roasting still made his coffee palatable.

It was a pity the coffee beans had to come such a long way, which was why they were so terribly expensive. The price

14

was a bit better these days. Now that coffee was being grown in Arabia, one did not have to go to Ethiopia for it. He wondered whether coffee might be grown efficiently in Brazil. When he had more time, he would investigate the possibility.

What a magnificent place this part of the New World was! Excellent weather. A choice of terrain—plains and mountains, all within a day's journey. A variety of vegetation which a scholar would require a lifetime to classify. Adequate rainfall for growth. Unspoiled. Vast. Room for all of Europe in this New World, he mused. If only the authorities would understand and provide him with the men and materials he needed to really establish this foothold! And if only his colonists had been content! He could not understand the bickering and the nagging of those bloody Huguenots.

True, he had said he would not think of them again today. But who could put them out of mind?

It was his fault. He had invited them. He had enlisted them. He had brought several Hugenots with him when he first came to this place three years ago.

He had known some of them in France. He knew they had originally been known as partisan fighters from the Canton of Geneva, fighting under the banner of some warrior named Besançon Hugues. He knew, further, that these soldiers of fortune had accepted Calvin's reformed faith and eventually left French speaking Geneva for France, where they grew in numbers and wealth and prestige, where their beliefs spread rapidly, especially among the merchants and the educated.

They were good people. Certainly they were good workers. They were men and women of integrity and highest morals. But they were so proud and fanatical. So sure of themselves!

He tore what remained of the loaf of bread.

Looking back, he should never have allowed anyone to talk him into bringing prisoners as colonists three years ago.

15

Much as he now hated them, he should have been content with the Huguenots. Things might have worked themselves out. But he had to bring the prisoners from Paris and Rouen. And a few, even, from Orleans, from the south, which was not good. A few were fairly good artisans, but mostly they had come to the New World to enjoy themselves. On the one hand he had a fanatically religious people; and on the other, thieves and trollops. Mutiny and civil disorder were inevitable. Of course he had crushed it. With loss of blood and life.

And that was when he wrote Master John Calvin. Why did he do it? Whatever possessed him? Baring his soul to the reformer as he did, requesting more Huguenots and a minister to establish a church and restore moral order within the colony!

He winced as he remembered how he had signed his letter: "Your most loving and eager servant, from the heart!"

To be sure, they had exchanged letters before. And as an educated man he was aware of the rapid changes taking place within the church. Within his lifetime, within thirty years, the Church of Rome was shaking in an earthquake of upheaval and might yet fall. He knew of Luther, Zwingli, Farel, and Calvin. He knew of their preaching, although he was now of the opinion that the truth lay elsewhere.

How would it end? His Scottish guards were talking about some firebrand named John Knox, a priest like Luther, who was wreaking havoc in the northern kingdom. And the admiral knew Scotland well. He had commanded and led four ships, loaded with supplies, to help the lady from Lorraine, Mary of Guise, and her daughter, Mary Stuart. This Knox had organized the lords into some sort of covenant against the crown. The admiral frowned. He liked Scotland. He adored the crown. For his work he had been granted the rank of vice admiral, and at that time he retained the Scottish Guards, who still served him with loyalty.

16

Ten months ago more than four dozen new colonists had arrived, among them not one but two pastors, sent by John Calvin himself to establish a bridgehead of the Reformed faith in the New World.

Pierre Richier, an old but still able man, was a former monk of the Carmelite Order and a doctor of theology.

Guillaume Chartier, a Breton, thirty years of age, had studied at Calvin's Academy in Geneva.

And there were others: André La Fon, a wonderful tailor; Pierre Bourdon, a carpenter, cabinetmaker, and woodturner; an ironworker named Verneuil; and a former storekeeper called Balleur. He liked these artisans.

But the pastors constantly interfered.

And two other persons among those new arrivals thoroughly complicated his life.

There was Philippe de Corquillerary, known also as du Pont. He was one of the original Genevan mercenaries, who had likely served under Hugues himself. He was a nobleman. Without a doubt, he was the best qualified military man in the entire colonial contingent. The admiral sighed. He had underestimated this du Pont.

And there was Jean Bourdel. The admiral bristled at the memory of this schoolmaster who knew no useful trade, whose arrogance paraded itself in disputations of faith and theology.

But they were gone. They were now returning to France. He must remember that fact and rejoice! And Olaria—that festering pimple on the mainland, where a few renegades thought they lived beyond his ability to govern! Well, it would soon receive the attention it had long deserved.

But why should he distress himself in this manner?

The worst of the lot were gone! He was free of them!

Pastor Chartier, that boy preacher, left six months ago.

And du Pont, Pastor Richier, Bourdel, and the rest of them were well on their way back to France on the *Jacques.*

The admiral concentrated on the papaya, savoring its pleasant sweetness.

Of course, there was still much to be done. The island fortress had to be finished before the rainy season began this fall. The Portuguese were arriving more frequently and in larger numbers in the north and in the south, and his spies told him their fortifications were to be respected. Fort Coligny was essential to the security of France in this New World. The rains would soon come; and the deluge would halt the work, again, for another three months.

All he lacked were men and materials.

The materials were close enough for the taking, for the hauling.

And so were the men. There were Frenchmen, still living in Olaria, less than a mile away, on the mainland. He had to convince them to return to the island. He needed bodies to lift the timber and move the rocks.

He stood, rising slowly and stretching his heavy arms. He walked toward his window, adjusting the shutters, looking across the bay toward Olaria.

He would go to the renegade settlement today. He would talk to those Frenchmen. He could and he would contain his anger. He would be cautious. The men there knew he had little food and money to offer, so he would not promise too much.

No, the only appeal he could make would be an appeal to patriotism. They must rejoin the citadel—they must finish the citadel—because France was now in danger from the growing presence of Portuguese. Every Frenchman was born with love of country. His appeal would be to that love.

If he could win back even five men—that could make the difference in finishing the fort before the rains began.

"Tupí!" he called.

She appeared instantaneously, magically, beautifully.

He placed his arm around her waist and drew her to him.

18

He would, of course, go to Olaria—but later in the morning.

"Monsieur, you are hurting me!" she said, as she reacted to the pain.

In causing that pain, the admiral felt exhilarated.

3. La Fon

"Praise be to God who refreshes us with sleep!" said Jean Bourdel.

I confess that not all of us were eager to praise God with the sunrise. But each of us had slept well, and the fruit had given us much needed nourishment. We had found some new strength with which to begin a new day and resume our march back through the forest whence we had come.

"It always goes faster when you retrace your steps," said Matthieu. And I agreed. I had always found it so. Granted, there were few landmarks in a forest, but it seemed that we recognized clearings of land or clusters of growth which we had observed the day before, and the going was hastened.

By sunset we had crossed the peninsula and faced the ocean. We were fortunate that our sense of direction led us to within ten minutes of where we had beached our frail boat.

It was a miserable looking craft, and I wondered how we had been able to survive five days on the high seas. We had left the *Jacques* so quickly that the sailors forgot to give us a mast and a sail. Thus we had journeyed by rowing and later by improvising an oar into a mast, using our tattered shirts as sails.

We were tired and decided we would not resume our voyage until the following dawn. I think each of us dreaded setting foot inside the vessel.

"I think we should have walked around the bay instead of trying to stay afloat in this sinking boat!" said Pierre.

"It would have taken several days," said Bourdel, "to walk around the entire bay."

"And who knows what is at the north end!" said Matthieu. "I have never been there."

"There are Indian tribes," Jacques declared, "that much I know."

"Very well," said Pierre, "we shall sail, but I hope my hands will survive."

Each of us took our turn at the oars, making slow progress. We headed south toward the entrance to the bay, rowing against a strong current. We had long since given up our improvised sails; our shirts were not fit even to serve as rags.

"We must be careful of the Portuguese!" said Jean.

"Nonsense," I said. "They have a colony to the south of us at Saint Vincent. It would take a week to sail there. And Salvador, to the north, is a month away."

"There are more of them than there are of us," said Jean Bourdel. "They arrive in greater numbers, and who knows where they colonize. And we must remember that our countries are at war."

Jacques burst out laughing. "As God's chosen people, we have been given strange choices. Burial at sea. Starvation on land. Capture by the Indians or the Portuguese!" He continued to laugh.

"Don't exclude the choice of returning to Coligny!" I joined him in the laughter, suddenly realizing that it had been many weeks since I had heard anyone laugh. Villegaignon had taken away our capacity to laugh.

"I'll never return to Coligny!" said Jacques softly but firmly.

Escape from our world of unhappy choices had seemed to be so promising of success only a fortnight ago.

We thought the caravelle named *Jacques* was a sturdy vessel when we had boarded her in Olaria. Many of us had helped to load her and make minor repairs. We knew she was an old ship and obviously a small ship. Nevertheless, she had crossed the Atlantic six times, and we had had no doubt that she would be able to make the return trip of her seventh crossing.

Five days later, on the open sea, du Pont discovered the first leak during a routine inspection he was making of the stores. He quickly found the captain.

"I don't want to cause panic," du Pont said, "but I think you should investigate."

Several of us joined them as they went below deck.

"Look," du Pont pointed. "The hull is rotten!"

"It is rotting, monsieur!" said the captain, "not rotten."

"Is there a difference?" du Pont asked. "Our lives are in danger!"

"Monsieur, you knew this was an ancient vessel when you boarded her. She sailed the Mediterranean for three dozen years before she first crossed the Atlantic. She is tired."

There was no way to hide the danger, and we soon formed

a bucket brigade, made up of crew and passengers. The leak was fast becoming an invasion, and the water was soaking our belongings and some of the food, particularly the supply of biscuits.

"We must reduce our weight if we are to survive," the captain announced.

"What do you propose?" asked our pastor, Pierre Richier.

"There are your belongings."

"But we have so little left. We sold most of what we owned to pay for our passage."

"You do have clothing, much of it wet and most of it, I fear, ruined. If we could eliminate a ton of weight, that would be a good beginning."

Pastor Richier looked carefully at each one of us. None raised an objection.

"So be it," he said.

The captain nodded his thanks. But he did not smile.

"I am very sorry, but more will have to be done." The captain began to pace back and forth, nervously.

"What do you mean?" asked our senior pastor.

"Some of you must return to the mainland. There are too many people aboard!"

This time, as Pastor Richier looked at us, he did hear objection. Our people had waited too long for an escape from the tyrant, Villegaignon. For a few moments, everyone seemed to be talking at once. Except the crew, of course. They stood about laughing or taunting us, quite certain that no crewmember would be asked to leave.

"How many should leave?" asked the pastor.

"At least five persons," the captain replied. "They may take the small boat. We would save another ton and a half, perhaps. In addition to the very important fact that five persons would not be eating our reduced food supply."

"I will be one of the five," said our pastor.

Jean Bourdel marched forward without hesitation.

"No, sir!" he said. "You must never return to the mainland. For you it would be too dangerous."

"I am an old man," said Pastor Richier. "I am not afraid of the danger. And my life does not matter."

"Sir, it matters that you return to France and explain to the authorities what has been happening here!" shouted Bourdel. We added our agreement. "You will be heard. You can explain the matter effectively."

The captain looked defeated and worried. "A decision must be reached quickly," he said.

"I volunteer to return to the mainland," said Bourdel. "I am unmarried. I have no close ties in France." He paused. "Who will join me?"

"I will," I said. "I am a widower and an old man, and I do not know if anyone would remember me in Le Havre."

Three others quickly joined us.

Jacques le Balleur and Matthieu Verneuil were bachelors. It seemed important to us that those with wives and families should remain with them.

And there was Pierre Bourdon. He was married.

"We have run out of bachelors and widowers," he said. Except for our pastor, it was a true statement. "Others are called upon to make a sacrifice. I will go!" Pierre declared.

His young wife began to cry softly and painfully, it seemed to me. Hers were tears of pride and great sadness.

There was only a moment for both of them to embrace and have a final word, because the captain was having the small boat lowered into the water. We were told to collect our belongings. Within a half hour, after a brief prayer led by our pastor, we were on our way.

As I mentioned, in this haste we were not provided with mast or sails, which were left on the *Jacques*. After our first day of limited progress, we used an oar for a mast and tied our shirts with our belts to that improvised mast, hoping to take advantage of the breeze.

The second day was uneventful, but on the third day we knew we were lost. We no longer could see the caravelle. Nor could we discern the mainland. And on that third day, a storm arose, continuing for a day and a half, tossing us about to where we despaired of being able to remain inside the boat. We had no food. Considering the roughness of weather and water, that was good.

The rain stopped during the night of the fourth day, and the fog lifted on the fifth. We saw land and beached our boat. We did not know where the storm had brought us, so we began to walk and explore. That was when we found the body of Carmeau and learned that we had returned to the place we had left only days before.

"We will proceed to Olaria," said Jean Bourdel.

"We have no choice," said Jacques.

We had now entered the bay and were staying as close as we could to the northern shore.

"I can make out Coligny!" shouted Matthieu.

"I know you have better eyesight than I do," I said, "but is yours that good?"

"Everyone's eyesight is better than yours, La Fon!" It was good to hear Bourdon laughing.

"But Coligny must be three leagues from here!" I said.

"I can make it out," said Matthieu.

"So can I," Bourdon agreed.

"There is risk in going to Olaria," said Jacques.

"You just said we had no choice," Bourdel said, rather impatiently.

"True," Jacques replied. "But it could be dangerous for us."

"It is not a part of the admiral's fort!"

"It is only a short distance from Coligny."

"Villegaignon cannot harm us there."

"His tentacles can reach that far, I think," said Jacques. "If he wants to do mischief, that slimy octopus can do his dirty work anywhere!"

Bourdel was silent for a moment.

"And the alternative, Jacques?" asked Bourdel finally.

"There is none."

"I think we can find lodging with Lery," I volunteered.

"That crazy writer?" asked Matthieu.

"He is an accountant. A bookkeeper!" I said.

"He fills his journals with words, not figures!"

"He keeps a record of events," I said. "Someday that record may be very important to the authorities!"

"What do you think, Bourdel?" asked Pierre. "What should we do?"

"I think we should keep our heads down and stay as far away from Coligny as we can!"

"I mean when we get to Olaria."

"I think La Fon has a good idea," said Bourdel. "Lery has room for us, I think. He has been a good friend. And he hates Villegaignon."

We lifted our oars and saw that a current was carrying us toward the mainland.

"Let's rest a while and stay with the current as long as we can," said Pierre.

"Of course, my friends, there is one all important thing for me in Olaria," said Bourdel. "I want to find another ship returning to France and somehow, some way, return with her!"

We added our amens spontaneously and fervently.

4. La Fon

"The admiral is in town!" Jacques threw down his cap on the table. "We're not here twenty-four hours, and Villegaignon shows his big face."

"A coincidence," I said.

Jacques snorted.

"Why is he here?" I asked.

"I did not stay around to inquire." Jacques went to the pottery urn to get some water. "It's miserably hot outside!"

"Drink slowly so you won't get á chill," I cautioned. "One sick comrade is enough."

"How is Pierre?"

"He still has a high fever. He's asleep in the hammock in the shade outside."

"Good," grunted Jacques. "Our strongest and tallest comrade gets the fever!"

"So the rest of us should be careful," I said.

"Where are the others?" he asked.

"Jean and Matthieu are looking for some kind of herb. They want it for Pierre, for a tea which is supposed to reduce fever."

"Is Lery with them?"

I nodded yes. It was brutally humid and hot inside the hut, and I was beginning to feel I had little energy for anything. I hoped I was not coming down with whatever illness had attacked Pierre.

"Is there anything to eat?" asked Jacques.

"There is fruit. Some mangoes."

"What will you be cooking for tonight?"

"Fish and manioc root."

"The same old thing!"

"It is food, Jacques. We should be grateful."

He pulled out his knife and began peeling a mango. He did not appear to notice when the others returned.

There was Jean Bourdel and Jean Lery. And Matthieu, of course.

"We found the herb," said Matthieu, as he handed me a small packet.

"You should boil it for at least ten minutes," said Bourdel. "Make it as strong as you can."

I stirred up the coals in the open pit stove, poured some water into a pot, and placed about half of the contents of the packet into the water. The herb tea smelled quite fragrant, something like chamomile.

"The admiral is back in town," said Jacques, throwing the mango seed through the open doorway.

"We saw him," said Bourdel.

"You saw him!" Jacques exclaimed. "Did you talk to him?"

"No," said Bourdel. "We only saw him. From a distance."

"He is as fat as ever!" said Matthieu.

"For him there is no shortage of food," said Jacques. "Why is he here in Olaria, Jean?"

"I heard rumors that he is looking for workers."

"For the fortress?"

"Yes."

Jacques laughed.

"Did Villegaignon see you?" I asked.

"I'm sure he did not," said Lery. "I'm sure he doesn't know you are even here."

"Don't count on that!" said Jacques.

"If he doesn't know we're here, someone will soon tell him," said Bourdel. "In that regard I am as cynical as Jacques."

"But I'm sure he did not come to Olaria today because he heard that five Huguenots had returned!" Lery affirmed with some vehemence.

Jean Lery was an accountant who had worked in one of the banking establishments of Geneva. He was thirty years old. He loved to write. He kept daily journals and records of events. He was our historian, and much later he gave me some encouragement to put down my own memories in the form of words and sentences. Lery dreamed of writing books and yet, for all of his hatred of Villegaignon, had been content to remain in Olaria when the rest of us set sail. As things turned out, it was just as well he had not gone with us. And, happily for us, he had given us lodging in his hut.

"Was Villegaignon alone?" asked Jacques.

"He had his usual retinue—the three Scottish guards."

Jacques spat into the fire.

"Careful of the tea!" I shouted. And then I laughed.

"Sorry," said Jacques, unsmiling. "Those skirt wearers make me want to vomit."

"They are called kilts, not skirts," said Bourdel.

"And they are formidable fighters," added Matthieu. "Of all people, Jacques, you ought to know that."

"They are weaklings!" he said.

"They are strong men," I said. "And even brave, I suppose."

"Why does he have the foreign skirts to protect him?" argued Jacques.

"Because Villegaignon is shrewd," said Lery. "He must have bodyguards who are loyal. The Scotsmen don't speak very much French and don't fully understand what's going on. All they know is that the admiral once helped their queen. So they are loyal."

"You might say they serve his purposes admirably," I said, hoping my pun would bring some levity to our ponderous conversation. Instead, it evoked scowls.

By this time the tea had been boiling for several minutes, and it smelled good. Surely it would do Pierre no harm, and it might even help him. I almost dropped the pot because it was so hot. Bourdel threw me a rag.

"If he's awake, we have things to discuss together," he said.

Pierre was awake, but he was very weak. His head was warm, even to my hand which had been nearly burned. He was running a high fever still.

"How goes it, Pierre?" asked Bourdel.

Pierre raised his hand slightly, in a kind of wave, but said nothing.

"Here is some tea for you," I said. "It's some kind of herb. Let me hold the cup for you while you try to drink."

"Pierre," Bourdel began, "Admiral Villegaignon is here in Olaria."

I felt Pierre's muscles tense.

"We don't think he saw us. But I think we may expect a visit from him. Perhaps quite soon."

"Jean, if you really think he will come, then we should escape! Now!" Jacques was on his feet.

"I don't think we have anything to fear."

"Jean, he hates all Huguenots!"

"And we are in Olaria, not Coligny."

"He has three guards with him now and other soldiers in the fort. We are at his mercy!"

"I think Jacques speaks much truth," I said. "Perhaps we should escape."

"It sounds so simple," Bourdel sighed. "Escape! Where? How? With what?"

"We still have the boat!" Jacques said.

"And we have no supplies. And we wear only the rags we have on our backs. And where would we go? To the Portuguese, with whom the French are at war? Or to the Indians, and be made slaves? And would Pierre be able to travel with us, with his fever and his weakness? It would be foolish to escape."

"And you advocate that we should remain here, simply hoping for the best?" Jacques was angry. "You say we should do nothing?"

"I did not say that. I do have a plan I wish to discuss with all of you."

"Jean Bourdel, you cannot trust Villegaignon. He will kill us!"

"Why?" asked Bourdel. "I grant you we are not his most popular subjects. But we are not criminals. We did secure his official permission to leave. A near disaster at sea brought us back. We broke no laws, and according to the admiral's own laws we should be treated fairly."

"Jean, you trust that man too much!" said Jacques.

"Bourdel, don't forget that Villegaignon makes the laws

here," said Lery, our host. "He changes the laws, too. We all know that. Whenever it suits his fancy, he changes the laws. So don't count on being treated fairly!"

"I will not believe the worst of any man!" said Bourdel.

"Then why did you decide to leave with the rest of us?" asked Jacques le Balleur. He was livid with anger.

"I decided to leave because I no longer could live in this place. And I still wish to return to France. However, I believe the admiral has absolutely nothing to hold against us. Even by his laws! And so I say we have nothing to fear. At least for the present."

"Jean, let me ask you something," I said. "Why does the admiral employ an executioner? Or maintain a prison? Or keep a room full of implements of torture? We've seen these things! We haven't dreamed them. This man is a tyrant. And he enjoys being cruel. Besides, we do know that he hates us!"

"I'm sure he would say that he keeps his prison for prisoners who break the law."

"His law, Jean."

"Very well," said Bourdel. "And the reality for us is that we somehow must survive all of this. I think we can, even with a a fiend like the admiral."

"I thought you just said you would not believe the worst of any man!" said Jacques.

"The reality of Villegaignon is bad enough without making it any worse. I think we can survive all of this if we keep our wits about us. With God's help we can do it!"

As we pondered alternatives, we seemed to be overcome with a sense of depression and hopelessness.

"Comrades!" shouted Bourdel. "Listen, there is one thing each of us shares."

We looked intently at Bourdel.

"Each of us desires, somehow, to return to France!"

Pierre clasped my hand to indicate his agreement.

"Even you, Lery, would agree to that now, wouldn't you?" Bourdel asked.

"I would prefer to return to my canton of Geneva, rather than France," he said. "But I certainly agree with you in principle."

"Very good," said Bourdel. "We need a ship to return to Europe. The ships arrive here infrequently. Most of these are government vessels, and we know we have no hope of boarding such. The private caravelles occasionally hire sailors, but this is rare. We shall need to purchase passage, and for this we need money."

"And we don't have any money!" shouted Jacques. "What's your great solution, Jean?"

"We have nothing more to sell. We have nothing more to barter, except ourselves. We must find work."

"What about commerce?" I asked. "The privateers sail here looking for pepper corns, furs, Brazil wood. These things could buy us passage!"

"André," said Bourdel, "we still need money to buy the knives and axes and cloth with which to make trade with the Indians. It is still a question of money. And for money, we must work."

"Where?" asked Jacques.

"There is no work to be had in Olaria," said Lery. "The few artisans we have are employed, or merely existing."

"I know," Bourdel sighed. "I was asking about available work today."

"Then where is there work?" again asked Jacques.

"On the island."

"On Coligny?!"

Jean Bourdel nodded.

"You're out of your mind, Bourdel!" exclaimed Jacques.

"Villegaignon would never employ us!" I said.

"And if he would, I would never work for him!" said Jacques.

34

"Obviously he needs workers," said Bourdel. "That is why he came to Olaria today. To try to recruit Frenchmen who had left the island. He has to complete the fortifications!"

"He needs more than six men for that kind of task!" said Matthieu.

"Agreed!" Jean Bourdel replied. "But he needs all of the skilled artisans he can find. He can get common laborers much more easily, people to haul materials and supplies and do much of the work with proper supervision. Matthieu, you are an ironworker. Pierre, here, is an excellent cabinetmaker who knows carpentry."

"Pierre is sick; he cannot be moved!" said Jacques.

"Jacques, you were a merchant, but weren't you once a stonemason?" asked Bourdel.

"I was, and I have cut and laid stone on Coligny," Jacques answered. "But never again!"

"André, you and I do not possess these kinds of skills," said Bourdel, "but there are ways we can fill a need. You are a tailor and I was a schoolmaster. But we know something about surveying and laying foundations. We've done it— together!"

"I don't know, Jean," I said. "I don't like the idea. Why should we even offer ourselves to the admiral?"

"For two reasons. First, we need the employment to earn the money in order to return to our homeland. And, second, the fortification is important to France. In spite of all of the misunderstandings and even the tyranny of Villegaignon— we are still Frenchmen."

"How quickly you have forgotten, Jean Bourdel!" Jacques exclaimed. "Only a few weeks ago, Pierre Bourdon, who lies here so ill, was whipped by these Scottish henchmen, at the admiral's orders, for some wood carvings Pierre had made, on his own time, from wood he had cut himself, which he hoped to sell upon his return to France. You were standing there! You saw the injustice, the hatred, the stupidity of it

all! Not only was poor Pierre whipped, but the admiral confiscated Pierre's carvings. I have no doubt that Villegaignon
still has them or plans to sell them himself at his first opportunity. I am a Frenchman but not that much of a Frenchman
that I will work for such a man, a man who dishonors his
country as well as the navy uniform he wears!"

Pierre had been listening intently and nodded weakly as
Jacques spoke.

"We will, of course, vote on the matter as has been our
custom in regard to all important decisions," said Bourdel,
who appeared to be greatly fatigued. "What I am suggesting
is that we simply ask for employment; and if the admiral
agrees to this, we understand among ourselves that this is not
forever but only for a few short months, for only as long as is
necessary to secure the funds with which to purchase passage
back to France. What do you think?"

"I will never again work for the admiral!" said Jacques.

"Even if the rest of us should so decide?" asked Matthieu.

"Correct," Jacques declared.

"We have always followed the majority decision, Jacques,"
I said. "It has been our custom, our way of doing things!"

"In this instance, I will not follow our way," Jacques said.
"I'm sorry. But I will never again work for the admiral, under
no circumstances whatsoever."

"And the rest of you? How do you feel?" asked Bourdel.

We did not answer immediately. I was torn between the
two alternatives. I had seen enough of the admiral's temper
and cruelty. Since I often did my tailoring in his personal
quarters, I had seen things others had only heard about. He
often struck people with his hands and fists, but I had also
seen him strike people with a piece of heavy chain. I knew
how easily he would banish people from the island, people
who displeased him or who had committed some minor in-
fraction of his rules. Carmeau, whose corpse we had found in
the forest, had been one of these. There was a man in the jail

who had been there for two years, I had learned. He and others had been hungry and without food for a week, and had broken into the admiral's private stores. I did not like much of what I had seen in Villegaignon. I feared him. Still, I also saw the logic of Bourdel's argument: we did need to work and, at the moment, the only work seemed to be back on the island.

Reluctantly, I ventured my opinion that I thought our only choice was to ask the admiral for employment. Matthieu agreed with me. When we asked Pierre what he thought, he nodded his head affirmatively but sadly.

Jean de Lery, who had already lived for many months in Olaria, said he would continue to do so until he could find a way back to France. Besides, he said, he wasn't part of our group and it wasn't his decision. "You are welcome to stay in my hut, however," he added, "as long as you wish."

"Jacques, you will reconsider, of course?" asked Bourdel. Jean simply could not accept a negative answer!

"No," answered Balleur. "Not 'of course'! I'm sorry, Bourdel. We've been companions through many ordeals. I suppose I am alive today because we shared so many dangers together and because we helped each other. I am grateful to each one of you. But I will not serve the tyrant."

"What will you do?" I asked.

"I will find something to do. I have been a storekeeper. I ought to be able to make trade with the Indians. I will take my chances." He walked to the side of the hut, looking toward the bay.

"There will be time to talk about this tomorrow!" Bourdel said with a smile and his usual optimism.

"There is no time," replied Jacques with a frown, returning to our group. "Time has ended for us. The admiral and his guards are here."

5. La Fon

The admiral shifted his great girth on the rude bench we had given him, apparently in considerable discomfort.

"I trust each of you is in good health," he began.

"Except for Pierre Bourdon, we are all well," said Bourdel. "Pierre has contracted a fever."

"I regret to hear it," replied Villegaignon. "Bourdon is the turner, the cabinetmaker, is he not?"

Jean nodded. I thought to myself, *he is also the woodcarver whom you whipped.*

"Your return is quite unexpected," said the admiral, somewhat nervously. "I learned about it at the wharf today."

"And we only arrived yesterday, excellency," said Bourdel.

"How went the voyage?"

"The ship was overcrowded and overloaded, sire. Some fifteen leagues from shore we began to take water. Much of the food was ruined. It was decided that five of us should return to conserve what food was left and to reduce the weight of the vessel."

"And you were the five who were chosen?"

"Yes."

"And your comrades? How do they fare?"

"We pray that they fare well, excellency. We left in considerable haste, and we did not see the *Jacques* after the second day. It is an ancient vessel."

"Yes, I know. And you came in that little bark I saw at the wharf?"

"Yes, sire."

"With no mast?"

"With no mast, sire."

You had to give the man his due. He was extremely observant and he had a fantastic memory.

"Wasn't Bourdon, your turner, married?" Pierre nodded weakly. "And your wife is on the *Jacques?*" Pierre closed his eyes for a moment.

"La Fon, I am delighted to see you again, to be perfectly honest!" The admiral beamed at me. I bowed slightly and gave him a half smile in return. Villegaignon was certainly trying to be friendly.

"Well, despite the surprise of your return, I do give thanks to Almighty God for your safety." He seemed to mean what he said, but who can truly judge such matters except God? "And what will you do now? What are your plans?"

"I trust somehow that our Lord Jesus Christ will prepare a way for our return to France," said Bourdel.

"The Lord Jesus?" Villegaignon smiled. "You still talk like a Huguenot, Bourdel!"

"Our lives are committed to Him, sire. You are aware of that. And your excellency knows that we desire to return to our homes in the Old World."

"And how do you propose to do this?"

"We will wait for some other ship."

"And how will you do this? It will take money."

"And we have no money, sire. In fact, we carry the remainder of our possessions upon our persons. We shall have to find work." Bourdel paused a moment, quickly glancing at the rest of us. "Perhaps you would find it possible to employ us?"

The admiral seemed quite surprised at the suggestion.

I caught a glimpse of Jacques who was now standing next to the hut, some distance away from our group. His lips were thin and taut. And his eyes were cold and bitter.

"I must, of course, remind you that you did leave the fortress under rather strange circumstances," Villegaignon said.

"Excellency, throughout our stay in New France we have hidden nothing. There has been no secrecy. We left Coligny openly. We negotiated with the ship's captain openly—and with you for permission to leave."

"True."

"And you see, excellency, that we have returned to this place and to your jurisdiction openly, not in secret. Our consciences are clear."

"It is a good point."

"We were not deported by your excellency. You allowed us to leave, freely. You said we had completed our obligation. We are citizens of France. We are Christians. You know that we are trustworthy and that we are good workers."

"And you are also Huguenots. I have not forgotten that fact!" The admiral seemed amused with some passing thought. "You left my jurisdiction because you were Huguenots."

"Because there were differences of opinion regarding the mode and manner of worship!" I sighed to myself, hoping that Jacques would not start an argument. However, Villegaignon was still smiling.

"There are questions to be resolved. I have submitted those questions and issues to the scholars in France. We do not need to review them until we hear from the masters of the Sorbonne!"

"Sire, the sea has claimed all that we own. We are victims and we request only what any victim of war or disaster would ask. In our case," said Bourdel with much eloquence, "we desire only to earn the means with which to return to the homeland."

Villegaignon rose from the bench slowly. He looked at each of us carefully and intently.

"I said I gave thanks to Almighty God for your safety. And I mean that with all my heart. Even though I am a sailor, I pray to God that I may never die at sea!" He walked to Jean Bourdel. "We have had our differences, Bourdel, but I am ready to forget the injuries of the past. Let God take vengeance if He will. Even if you were my enemies, I would still offer you hospitality. And I do not consider you to be my enemies."

Bourdel started to respond but thought better of it and remained silent. I suspect we were all amazed at the turn the admiral's speech had taken.

"There is one thing I must request however," Villegaignon resumed. "I do not object to your private devotions but I do ask that you keep your religious convictions to yourselves. I would object to any public worship in your Reformed tradition at this particular time." He was smiling and he was speaking softly. "There could be serious consequences if we

41

returned to the way things were before we hear from the Sorbonne."

It was a threat but it was said so quietly and so politely that we did not immediately recognize it.

"In every other way, you have the prerogatives and the liberties of Frenchmen!"

He started to walk away, then stopped.

"I think it will be possible to find employment for all of you. I will send you word at the appropriate time. And I hope your comrade gets better. Good day!" And with a flourish of his hat, he was gone.

We were silent for a minute or two.

"Where is Jacques?" I asked suddenly. "He was standing next to the hut!"

No one had seen him leave.

"What do you make of the admiral's pretty speech, Bourdel?" asked Matthieu.

"He seemed unusually pleasant."

"There were moments when I could not believe Villegaignon was speaking," said Jean Lery, our host.

"He restricts our worship," I said.

"And there was a threat," said Lery.

"I almost missed it," Bourdel smiled, "but I heard it. Still, on the whole, he was quite generous."

We heard someone running up the footpath behind our hut, but from the direction of the wharf.

It was Jacques le Balleur, rushing in and breathing hard.

"Come see what that bloated whale has done!" He pulled us toward the front of the hut, where we could see the bay. "See!" he shouted.

We looked in the direction he pointed. And we saw our bark, the small boat which had brought us to Olaria, being towed back toward the fortress on Coligny.

"He confiscated our boat, Bourdel!" Jacques grabbed Jean's arm in anger. "Before he came to see us, before he began all of this honey talk, he had confiscated our boat! That's the kind of man, the kind of liar, with whom you think you can work and negotiate!"

6. Villegaignon

The admiral was not in a happy mood.

The return trip to the island had been miserable. The bay was choppy and the long boat was, as always, uncomfortable. The sailors were combating wind and current, but not even his threats of a thorough flogging seemed to affect their rate of progress.

To add to everything else, there had been a summer shower which completely drenched everyone.

The admiral felt as though he had swum the bay as he debarked. He stepped on an oarsman's foot as he left and was delighted with the cry of pain he evoked. There were times when he truly enjoyed his rage.

A Scots guard saluted as he jumped ashore.

"Get word to La Faucille and Gardien. I must see them immediately. In my quarters."

The guard again saluted.

Tupí, his Indian slave, stood several paces away, smiling shyly.

"Prepare some tea, girl!" he shouted. "There's too much fever about and I am soaking wet!"

He changed into dry clothes quickly.

He paced the floor in his sitting room, awaiting the arrival of his aides. He stopped to look across the bay toward Olaria. The rain was ending, and the sky would soon be clear and blue again. If he had waited an hour, he would not have been caught in the summer squall. He thought of the men, those bloody Huguenots, whom he had seen. He picked up a feather duster Tupí had left in the room, placed it in his two mammoth ham-like hands, and, staring at Olaria, broke the handle in two, muttering an oath.

La Faucille arrived first. He was tall and thin and gave the impression of constant apprehension, as though he expected a poisonous snake to appear. La Faucille was now the garrison commander, ever since the Huguenot, Thoret, had been forced to give up his command.

"Is Gardien coming?" Villegaignon asked.

"Yes, your excellency!"

Gardien was a blacksmith, who now doubled as both jailer and executioner.

"Perhaps you have heard that they have returned?" asked Villegaignon, huskily.

"I heard that five Huguenots returned, yes," La Faucille replied. "Is Thoret with them?"

"Thoret, Thoret! What is it with this Thoret? You always ask about him! You are obsessed with the man!"

"Excellency, he was the commander before me!" La Faucille shifted his feet nervously. "After we had our fight, if you had not insisted on such a punishment—"

Villegaignon was holding one end of the feather duster handle he had broken and, walking briskly, went to his commander and hit him in the face with the broken stick. A red welt appeared immediately on La Faucille's left cheek.

"Do not question my judgment, Faucille!" shouted Villegaignon. "Never! And stop worrying about that piece of Reformed dirt." La Faucille was still rubbing his cheek. "Thoret has not returned. Besides he never left on that ship. If you remember, he escaped on a raft and God only knows where he is now."

"I dream that he is still alive, close by, and that he will return to whip me!"

"Then you dream too much! And start acting like a commander!"

Gardien entered with a knock and a bow. Although he was not a hunchback, he had been born with a slight deformity in his shoulder which sometimes gave people that illusion. His grotesque appearance was always accentuated when he wore the executioner's black hood. Villegaignon often smiled when he thought of Gardien; and he was smiling now, seeing him in the flesh. People were naturally frightened of Gardien. He made a superb jailer.

"Sit down, both of you!" the admiral commanded.

"How many did you say returned, excellency?" La Faucille asked.

"Five."

Gardien was bewildered.

"I take it you haven't heard," Villegaignon said. "Five Huguenots, five of the sixteen who left a fortnight ago on the caravelle, have returned. They are in Olaria."

"Which five?" Gardien inquired.

"Bourdel, Verneuil, Bourdon, La Fon, and Balleur." The

admiral spat out their names. "They're troublemakers. Especially Bourdel."

"He is a hardnosed one," La Faucille agreed.

"What happened? Did the ship sink?" Gardien asked.

"They say the ship proceeds toward France."

"It wasn't a ship I would like to travel."

"They said they returned in order to lighten the vessel, that it had begun to draw water."

"It is possible," said Gardien.

The admiral returned a look of disbelief.

"You saw them, excellency?"

"This morning."

"And how are they?"

"All except Bourdon are well. Bourdon is sick with a fever, which serves him right after trying to cheat me by smuggling out those carvings he had made, from wood he had cut for me!"

La Faucille and Gardien said nothing, waiting for Villegaignon's rage to subside.

"They had quite a story to tell," the admiral continued, "about hardship. About losing all they possessed. About wanting to secure work in order to pay for passage to France." He looked squarely at his lieutenants. "Naturally, I believe not one single word of what they said."

The two men were confused.

"What do you think happened?" La Faucille asked, finally.

"I think that their caravelle is within three or four days of here, anchored, and waiting for some word."

"A word of what?" asked Gardien.

"The word to return. The word from these spies!"

"Spies?" La Faucille shook his head. "Excellency, they are many things, perhaps, but spies?"

"Spies!" shouted the admiral. "This entire affair is a plot. I should have seen through it at the outset."

"With all due respect, sire, you did grant permission to the sixteen Huguenots to leave."

"What choice did I have? A captain, not under my employ nor jurisdiction, who owns his own vessel, agreed to take them for one hundred escudos. They found the money somehow, and ultimately I had to give the captain permission to sail. Who knows what kind of a report he would have carried to France and to the court had I refused? Besides, it looked to me like a sinking tub, and I really hoped the whole lot of them would drown!"

"I still do not understand the nature of the plot," La Faucille said. "I would like to understand."

"Very well. We begin with Pastor Richier. He is the master mind of the plot."

"He is an old man, excellency!"

"He may be old, but he is still strong and he is devilishly clever. He loves power—just like that John Calvin who took over the city of Geneva. These priests and preachers are all alike. It was Richier who threatened me and my government. And don't forget that du Pont is with them. That fox of a soldier!"

"But what is the plot, sire?"

"Richier is on that caravelle, on the *Jacques,* perhaps less than a dozen leagues from here. The ship may have been old but I don't believe this story of five men leaving to save a ship! Five men would not make that much difference. No, this was the plot: to send back five men to pretend to be survivors of a disaster who would gradually infiltrate the garrison and gain support here and in Olaria. When the proper moment arrived, they would get word to the caravelle so that Richier and the others would return in time to make a success of the revolt!"

"Ingenious, mon admiral!" said Gardien.

"I shall cancel all leaves and we'll strengthen the guard. No one will take this fortress," La Faucille affirmed.

48

"Make everything secure, take every precaution!" Villegaignon said. "Including the jail, Gardien! We have several Huguenot prisoners, do we not?"

"Four at the moment, excellency."

"These spies would surely try to release their comrades. All remaining Huguenots must now be suspect!"

"What else can be done, sire?" La Faucille asked.

"I have confiscated their boat, and it has been brought back to the island. And I left word in Olaria that no one was to lend them a boat, under penalty of death!"

"This is to keep them from contacting Richier, at sea."

"Precisely."

"When you saw them today, how did they receive you?"

"I think I surprised them with my visit. But they had no choice; I am the commander in chief. And I think I put on a very good show," Villegaignon laughed. "I think I convinced them that I was truly glad to see them, happy they had survived their ordeal. Then that sly rat of a schoolmaster, Bourdel, gave their plot away."

"How so, excellency?" Gardien asked.

"He asked that they be allowed to work for me again. Here on the island!"

"No Huguenot in his right mind would want to do that!" La Faucille roared, then stopped and reddened, beginning to stutter as he saw the admiral's glare. "Obviously, this was part of their plan, to return to the island! Even though everyone knows they have no more love for you than you do for them!"

"Faucille, you do have a brain!" the admiral snorted. "Of course they must come to the island in order to complete their plan, and somehow they learned I was looking for skilled workers. But what they don't know is that I am aware of their plan, and have one of my own."

"And your plan, excellency?"

"I also want them on this island. I can handle them more

easily and effectively here than if they stay in Olaria. If we maintain proper surveillance here, they will never be able to contact their comrades on the caravelle!"

"Will you give them work?"

"I will offer them work. I will promise them work. But as soon as they set foot upon the island, I will have them jailed!"

"Jailed?" Gardien asked.

"I will want them chained. We have sufficient chains for five more prisoners?"

"But of course, excellency."

"Under what pretext will you jail them, sire?" La Faucille inquired.

"That, too, is part of my plan. These Huguenots are a strange lot. They think too much, they argue too much, among themselves and with others. But they have one thing in common which, for them, is the supreme thing in their lives; it is their faith. That faith is not only being subjected to serious questioning by the authorities in France by way of questions I have sent, but that faith already has been considered heretical in several places."

"I do not understand, excellency," said La Faucille. "For what reason would they be jailed?"

"They would be jailed as heretics. As confessed and convicted heretics!"

"How will that occur, excellency?"

"I told you I had a plan. You will see, these Huguenots will return to the island voluntarily. They will think they are using me, that they are deceiving me—but they will fall into my trap."

La Faucille and Gardien were smiling.

"You see, my trusting lieutenants, I am still the representative of his most Catholic Majesty Henry and I am responsible for maintaining the purity of the most holy Catholic faith at his majesty's colony at Coligny!"

7. La Fon

I succumbed to whatever illness it was which continued to plague Pierre. I felt like a pendulum of a clock, swinging from chill to fever, not caring if I would ever see the dawn of another day.

At times I was aware of people coming in and out of the hut. I remember drinking various mixtures of herbs, but I cannot remember eating any food. I now know that Pierre had made no recovery and was still fighting his own fever, but at the time I was conscious of very little.

Although I was physically conscious of little, throughout my illness my mind was far from dormant. I have heard it said that people facing death relive all of their past, much of it with great rapidity. I suspect I may have been close to death. And I did relive much of my past, especially the excitement and the horror of the past twelve months.

There were times when it did not seem possible that we had been in Brazil for only a year. It seemed more like a decade since we had sailed from Honfleur, in Normandy.

I was a widower of a very few weeks. My dear Mathilde had died quite unexpectedly. I suppose that could be said of most deaths.

I truly expected to die before she did. She had always been healthier. I was the one who suffered from colds and asthma and rheumatism. But early in September, two years ago, she was thoroughly drenched in a rainstorm and caught a severe cold which caused lung congestion. Two weeks later she was dead.

We had been married for thirty-two years. And we had had a good life. I remembered those better days, in my fever, with great relish and delight. The time we went to Rouen to see the place where Joan of Arc died. We marveled like children at the delightful musical clocks which arched the streets. The times we picked apples together in our beautiful Norman orchards. Apples! I could taste them on my parched lips—but none of us in Brazil had even seen an apple for months. For the earliest settlers, it had been several years.

Our two children were married and had their own families. So after Mathilde's death I was quite alone. And lonely. I kept staring at the shingle swinging in the wind outside my window:

ANDRÉ LA FON
TAILOR

And I had always been proud of the careful work I had done.

Work was still something to do, to occupy time. But the joy in my work had fled with Mathilde's passing.

I lived in Le Havre. Honfleur was a port of equal size across the bay, which body of water farther south became the river Seine. I enjoyed meeting captains and navigators and sailors who had journeyed to distant places. Through them, I learned of the larger world beyond France.

So it was that when Pastor Pierre Richier and his party arrived to make final arrangements for their journey to Brazil, I was recruited almost before I was asked.

"Monsieur La Fon, we shall need a tailor in Brazil!" beamed Pastor Richier. "Why don't you join us?"

And why not? I felt an excitement I had not thought I would ever feel again. I decided on the spot. Fortunately—or providentially, as Pastor Richier would put it—I had received an offer for my tailoring shop only a few days before. It was a good offer and the buyer was still interested. So there was nothing to hold me. No family. No shop.

However, before I could be officially accepted it was necessary to be interviewed. Philippe de Corquillerary was assigned to me.

"You must call me du Pont," he said. "Everyone else does and it is much easier to pronounce than Corquillerary!"

"Agreed," I said, laughing with du Pont.

I learned that he was a military officer and a Genevan. He was quite close to John Calvin who had asked him to assume major responsibility in organizing this expedition.

"I need to question you regarding your faith, monsieur La Fon," he began, "unless you consider this a private matter?"

"No, sire," I said. "I shall try to answer you. It is a strange way to begin an interview of this kind, I would think."

"You know that we go to Brazil."

"Of course."

I had lain awake for two nights thinking about everything I had heard about Brazil. And I had learned much from the mariners in our two ports. Exotic plants, tropical fruits, elegant hard woods, strange natives! I knew that Cabral had discovered Brazil more than fifty years ago and, because he was Portuguese, Portugal was busily colonizing that land on the northern coast and in the south. I knew also that even though Cabral had visited and named the area to which we would be traveling, the Rio de Janeiro, the Portuguese had not yet settled in that place.

"We go to a new colony of France, named Coligny," said du Pont.

Gaspard de Coligny was head of the admiralty in Paris.

"And we go at the specific request of the governor of that colony, Admiral Villegaignon."

I had heard many stories of the exploits of the admiral.

"The colony has been in existence for two years, and more colonists are needed. People of special skills and capabilities. And the admiral has especially asked that these new colonists be of the Reformed faith. He sent his request to Geneva, to Master John Calvin."

"Pastor Richier told me about this, sire," I said.

"Do you know the Reformed faith?" du Pont asked.

"I have heard something of Huguenots."

"What do you know of them?"

"That they are French-speaking followers of John Calvin, who came to France from Geneva. Now all Calvinists in France are being called Huguenots."

"You know of John Calvin?"

"I have heard much of John Calvin!" I said. "There are people on both sides of the bay—here in LaHavre and in Honfleur—who discuss him and his teachings."

"And what do you know about John Calvin?"

"That he was a lawyer. That he studied theology. That he had a dispute with the masters at the Sorbonne. You know he was born not too distant from here—in Noyon, to our east!"

"Yes, I know."

"We have heard that Calvin wrote a large volume called *The Institutes of the Christian Religion."*

"How did you come to hear about that book? It is a formidable volume!"

"We have heard that the church authorities are not happy with it. And we felt it an oddity for someone who is not a priest to write about theology. A lawyer who discusses Holy Scripture!"

"And what do you feel is most important in Master Calvin's teaching?"

"I think it is what he shares with Dr. Luther of Germany."

"You know of Luther, also, in this place?"

"Sire, any seaport is the best place in the world to learn of new things! Anyway, I like what I hear about the need only to trust Jesus Christ and to follow the Scriptures."

"Are you a Huguenot, monsieur La Fon?"

"No, sire." I paused. "At least, I do not know if I am."

"A Lutheran?"

"No."

"What would you call yourself? Are you a Catholic in good standing?"

"I am a seeker of truth."

"Do you know what Master Calvin calls the church in Geneva?" I shook my head indicating that I did not know. "He calls it 'The Church of Jesus Christ, Reformed According To The Word of God.'"

"That is a very long name for a church!" I jested. Du Pont was not smiling and so I became serious. "So that is where your word Reformed comes from."

"Indeed."

"Then, perhaps, I too am Reformed!" I declared.

"Do not affirm that in haste, my friend," said du Pont. "We would enjoy having you with us and we need a man of your skills. But consider this matter carefully."

"I don't understand!" I said. "You want me to commit

myself and I am ready to do so! Truly!"

"Fine!" smiled du Pont, extending his hand to me. "We worship God at His table tomorrow." He was searching for something to write on and I gave him the tablet and chalk I used in tailoring. "Thank you," he said. "This is where we meet. Tell no one. But come."

I shook my head in bewilderment.

"We shall grow in our faith together!" said du Pont. "Au revoir."

I found the house the next day and was admitted quickly. There seemed to be a mystery or apprehension which saturated the small dwelling and the several dozen persons who were present. I recognized Pastor Richier, who nodded to me. Du Pont approached me with a young man at his side.

"You found us!" he said.

"But, of course!" I responded.

"I'm glad you came. I want you to meet Captain Denis."

I extended my hand. And it was then that I saw that Captain Denis had no hand.

"Don't be embarrassed," he said. "The Gospel says that if one's right hand offends, it should be cut off." He smiled wanly. I thought it was a very poor joke.

"You lost it in battle?" I asked.

"In a way."

"That Scripture was used by the people who cut off his hand, who thought him to be a heretic," explained du Pont.

"I do not recommend Mieaux as a place to visit," said the captain.

"I have heard rumors of such things but I did not believe them," I said.

"See that girl over there?" du Pont pointed. "Look at her forehead."

"The fleur-de-lis!" I exclaimed.

"Branded for her faith," he said. "You see, La Fon, this is

serious business for us. We Reformed Christians may be in peril of our lives—which is a very good reason for going to the New World. Tolerance for our way of believing is waning. Our way of faith, of believing, is dangerous. That's why I want you to be absolutely sure that you want to join us."

I nodded my thanks and found a place to stand, out of the way, where I could ponder what I had just seen and heard.

It was then that they came. Perhaps two dozen soldiers, breaking down the door, shouting "Heretics!" at the top of their lungs, and wielding their swords and knives.

The horror was brief but effective. The women and children scattered themselves, screaming. Several of the men resisted the intruders. I could not believe what I saw—that Frenchmen would treat Frenchmen in this way. I did not know if their purpose was to slaughter or merely to frighten.

After they were gone, leaving the communion table overturned, we counted our casualties. Several wounds and gashes, but apparently no broken bones.

But there was one fatality. Captain Denis had stood at the door and had tasted death by the sword. Captain Denis, who had no hand to share in greeting, but whose face I would never forget as I vowed in my white-haired age to be a good soldier for Jesus Christ.

We sailed from Honfleur on November 20, 1556, on three different vessels, all owned, we learned, by Admiral Villegaignon.

The smallest of the ships was the *Rosée,* on which sailed six boys and five girls with their matron.

Jean de Lery and his companions sailed on the *Sainte-Marie.*

Eighty of us sailed on the flagship, the *Petite Roberge,* whose captain was a nobleman named Bois-le-Compte, a nephew, it turned out, of Villegaignon.

My first impression was that the admiral was engaged in

some very productive and lucrative commerce.

My second impression was that the officers and the crew were accountable only to Villegaignon, and had only the vaguest kind of loyalty to our sovereign king of France.

Our voyage was notable for the many broken promises we experienced.

We were told there would be ample food—but food and water were rationed by December, before we reached the Canary Islands.

We were promised adequate quarters—but we men slept on deck to give the women and children what little space was available below.

We were assured that our ships were legitimate merchantmen, flying the flag of France as they did.

That illusion disappeared on January 6, 1557, the Holy Day of the Three Kings. In my province of France, this was the holiday on which we exchanged gifts, commemorating an earlier day when the Wise Men brought gifts to the Christ Child. But instead of gifts, we exchanged gunfire with a British ship, setting it afire.

"Why do we attack the English?" I asked a sailor.

He laughed in my face.

"We are not at war with the English!" I continued. "After so many years of fighting, we have finally agreed to peace!"

The sailor still refused to give me any explanation.

Two days later, we attacked a Portuguese ship. Perhaps this was a bit more justified, inasmuch as France was officially at war with Portugal. And on this particular voyage we were certainly quite aware of the fact that we were rivals, feverishly establishing footholds in the New World.

The Portuguese vessel was captured after a battle of six hours. The colonists all stayed below deck and the noise of the bombardment created much fear, especially among the children.

Weapons and supplies from the Portuguese ship were

transferred to ours. The Portuguese crew, those who were still alive, was placed in a long boat and set adrift. It was my impression that they were not given any provisions. Then our captain ordered a broadside leveled at the other ship, at close range, and it, of course, sank.

Pastor Richier and du Pont were furious.

"This was an outrage, captain!" declared du Pont. "Such treatment of prisoners is uncivilized!"

"Would you have preferred that I shoot them?" sneered the captain in reply.

"They were not given food or water! How will they survive?"

"You do not know that to be a fact, monsieur!"

"I have eyes with which to see, captain!"

"We do what we must."

"Such action is unworthy of France!"

"Now, monsieur, this is not for you to say," said le Compte. "You are not French. You are Genevan. Let the French be concerned with their own worth and honor!"

"Much to my sorrow, Geneva is now under the protection of France. And I say that your action does France no honor, sir!"

The captain waved his hand in a gesture of nonchalance.

"Captain," the pastor interceded, "we were told we would be transported on a merchantman. This ship is nothing but a man-of-war!"

"We travel where there is much danger. We must be armed."

"We have attacked two ships during a single week," said du Pont. "That, sir, is not using weapons for defense."

"I do not know how you used to fight your battles, monsieur, but I am a man of action. I ask questions afterwards, not before."

"Captain you are endangering the lives of more than a hundred people!"

"Have any of you been injured?" asked the captain. "The admiral promised only that he would transport you to Brazil safely and at no expense to your persons. I have a copy of the agreement. And it is being followed."

Pastor Richier and du Pont looked at each other in dismay.

"I have some advice for you Huguenots," said the captain in a cold tone of voice. "This is my ship and I will sail her as I see fit. And I take my orders from Admiral Villegaignon, whose ship this is. He happens to hate the English; he fought them for too many years and does not easily forget. So whenever we see a ship bearing an English flag, we have orders to fire. And whenever we can, we will obtain whatever weapons and provisions we can. How do you think the admiral has been able to build and secure what he has in Coligny? The government has given very little. And if we get wealth and weapons from the Portuguese, so much the better!"

The captain left us without an adieu.

"It's blatant piracy!" sighed du Pont.

Fortunately, there were no more battles on that voyage but we decided to take our own measures, our own precautions, in view of the reality of our situation.

We organized ourselves in order to provide round-the-clock guards. We especially were concerned about the safety of our women. The sailors were an unruly lot and after their daily ration of rum became much freer with their insults and obscenities. Du Pont and Thoret, both of whom had themselves commanded military forces, instructed us. We would protect ourselves.

Jean Bourdel and I became good friends. We had at least two things in common. We were both about the same age. And we had both lost our wives; he, however, had been a widower for less time than I.

Jean Bourdel had been a schoolmaster. However, he had studied much theology. In fact, he confided to me one day that were he younger, he would choose to be a pastor. At any

61

rate, he did not wait to establish a school in the colony; he held classes on the *Roberge* and sent lesson assignments to the *Rosée*. On our ship, at least, we saw how his school gave structure and brought laughter to the lives of the children.

Altogether, we were some one hundred persons. Artisans, craftsmen, two pastors, a schoolmaster, wives, and children.

Pierre Richier was one of the pastors, a man close to my age, a former monk of the Carmelite order, and a very kind man.

Guillaume Chartier was the second pastor, a graduate of the Sorbonne and John Calvin's Academy in Geneva. He was much younger than Richier and he had the enthusiasm and the incaution of youth.

We worshipped God twice a day. We had morning prayers before breakfast and vespers just after supper. We followed the same schedule on Sundays with the exception that on the Sabbath we had a worship service in the afternoon as well.

I had heard about Reformed preaching but now I was hearing it for myself. I liked it. I appreciated the logic and the basis in Holy Scripture. And I particularly enjoyed the hymns I was learning to sing—hymns we sang in French, not Latin.

To be sure, not everyone in our contingent was of the Reformed persuasion.

John Cointac was one of whom we knew very little, a man of considerable mystery. He admitted to being a graduate of the Sorbonne. He and Pastor Chartier often discussed the university. He was versed in church history; the humanities; and seemed familiar with theology, past and present. I learned many new facts from him. I learned about Erasmus of Rotterdam and how his translations and writings had affected the reformation. He told me about John Wycliffe of England and John Hus of Bohemia, who had read Wycliffe's writings, and who had been burned to death at Constance for his preaching. I learned about Cardinal Ximénez of Spain, who was greatly interested in returning the Holy Scriptures to the people. So much more had been happening than the general things we had heard about Luther and Calvin. The continent was truly in a time of rebirth and many changes were taking place.

Cointac was a good teacher and a good person with whom to talk. But he never showed his hand or his mind, never committing himself to some specific stance of faith.

Jean Bourdel raised the possibility with some of us one day that Cointac might be a Roman priest, traveling to the French colony in disguise, as a special representative of the court. We thought Bourdel was letting his imagination wander—especially when we began to notice how frequently Cointac found opportunities to converse with a very lovely young girl who was emigrating with her family from Rouen.

The voyage required nearly four months, but finally the journey came to an end. We arrived in Brazil on March the seventh, in the year of our Lord 1557. We had endured much: warfare, hunger, storms. Days with no wind at all, when we would travel less than twenty miles in twenty-four hours. Most of us vowed that never again would we subject ourselves to this kind of ordeal. But within a few short months, we were eager and ready to risk whatever perils the sea might offer in order to return to our homes.

The admiral prepared a great feast for us on the day of our arrival. After so many days of rationed food and water, we ate too much of fresh fruit and bread and roasted meats, and I think everyone of the new arrivals was sick that first night on Coligny.

The admiral impressed us with his enthusiasm. And we were impressed, also, with the dimensions and state of the fort. Du Pont and Thoret thought that it already was capable of providing significant defense—although the admiral told us, from the beginning, of things which needed still to be done. It was amazing to realize how much had been accomplished in something like two years.

There were other Huguenots here who had come with Villegaignon on his first voyage. Throughout this time they had been without a pastor and there was much laughter and crying as we asked each other questions. Some of us even renewed friendships.

The Lord's Supper, which is the term Huguenots use for "Holy Communion," was held for the first time on Coligny on March 21, 1557. I think that perhaps it was the first time a Protestant service of this kind was conducted anywhere in the New World. It was a day of great significance and joy, especially for me.

I remember when I approached the table. How different it was from Honfleur!

"Welcome, André La Fon!" said Pastor Richier. "This is the Lord's table and all are welcome to it who confess Jesus Christ as Lord. Never must we partake of these elements unworthily. Do you confess Jesus as Lord?"

"I do!" I said, as I felt a great warmth and love overwhelm me. No one had formally asked me to become a Huguenot but I felt I was now truly a part of this Christian family.

As I thought about the wonder of it all, I heard Pastor Richier ask Admiral Villegaignon the same question. I marvelled that a lowly tailor and the governor of a colony of France could share this same Table of the Lord.

The admiral stood up, hesitantly, and, I thought, with some embarrassment. He began to recite the Apostles' Creed in a nervous and rapid manner.

"I believe in God the Father Almighty, maker of heaven and earth, and in Jesus Christ, His only Son, our Lord!"

Pastor Richier grasped his hand; and as the admiral knelt, the pastor said, "Welcome to the Lord's Table, my brother."

I made friends that very first week with a man named

Gardien. He was a blacksmith and came from a place called Caudebec. I knew that town quite well since it was on the Seine on the way to Rouen. He had been to Le Havre and Honfleur many times. We were Normans, and in a sense, we had been neighbors!

Gardien was anxious to show me around. First, I had to see his shop.

"The admiral secures the very best of iron, you see!" he said. "There is more of it on the vessel which brought you, including some very fine cannon which I am to install!"

I did not then inform Gardien how we had come to have those cannon.

"What are these?" I asked, picking up something that looked like a clamp.

"Those are leg irons," he replied.

Gardien then showed me many other items related to incarceration. There were chains attached to cannon shot and various kinds of leg irons and hand irons.

"You see these iron grills?" he asked.

"They are made quite well!" I said.

"They are for the prison. For bars in the windows and doors."

"There is a prison on Coligny?"

"Indeed! It is the second best building, after the admiral's own quarters." Gardien insisted that I see the edifice.

"How many persons will the prison hold?" I asked.

"About fifteen," Gardien responded. "But the admiral wishes it enlarged so we can take care of twenty-five, should the necessity ever arise."

"Has the prison ever been filled?"

"Two or three times."

"For what reason are people placed in prison?" I asked.

"Various things. Public drunkenness or public fighting. Sleeping with an Indian woman. Failing to salute an officer. Stealing food or materials from the admiral's supplies. Refusing to work. These kinds of things!"

We walked back to Gardien's blacksmith shop.

"I take it that completing the jail is one of the admiral's projects?" I asked.

"Yes."

"For some reason, I did not expect that there would be such concern to have a prison."

"You must remember, André," Gardien said, "that many petty thieves and criminals were sent on the first voyage. They have been troublemakers."

"Have Huguenots ever been arrested?"

"There have been times," Gardien hesitated. "The admiral is a strong-willed man."

We stood for a moment, overlooking the bay.

"That is Olaria," he said, pointing to a cluster of huts on the mainland. It seemed quite close but farther than I would wish to swim.

"Who lives there?" I asked.

"It depends upon whom you ask," Gardien chuckled.

"I'm asking you, Gardien."

"Mostly, they are people who can't get along here on the island. I'm not sure there are as many criminals there as the admiral thinks. A bad apple here and there, perhaps. There are several Huguenots who prefer to farm rather than build fortifications. Several fishermen. A couple of traders. And monsieur Villegaignon keeps several soldiers there to maintain order and to report back to him."

"It is part of the colony, then?"

"Indeed! This is the fort, Coligny, and, as you can see, a very large settlement. Olaria, there on the mainland, is one of our new French villages."

"Perhaps the first of many," I said.

"Perhaps, my friend!" agreed Gardien. "Come, there is one thing in the back of my shop I did not show you."

It was an item of torture and Gardien was quite proud of it.

I suppose one had to admit that the workmanship was excellent.

It looked like a coffin, but it stood upright. Once you opened the hinged door, you saw the long spikes, five or six inches long, protruding from the back of the lid.

I was horrified by the thing but said nothing immediately.

"I only finished it this week!" said Gardien triumphantly.

"It is intended for human use?"

"But, of course, André!" he said. "You place a person inside, you close the door, and something is felt." Gardien laughed.

I thought the item and the reaction were both indecent.

"The admiral drew the plans himself. He said he had seen something like it in the Bastille, in Paris. Do you know what he calls it?"

I shook my head, having no idea.

"His little cheese-maker!" Gardien continued to laugh, unable to contain himself. "You see, you could make little holes, as in cheese! The governor, in his strange way, is a humorous man!"

"What reason has been given for this kind of thing?" I asked.

"The fact that it exists may create such fear that it will never have to be used." Gardien was no longer laughing. "That, at least, is what his excellency told me."

Even in my fever, I knew I was in Olaria, but I was not sure how I had returned to this place.

Somewhere in the recent past, somehow, we had decided we could no longer remain in the colony. But events were not clear in my troubled and feverish mind.

My dreams became a nightmare of a mixture of beatings, arguments, seasickness, rotting food, and vomit. And above it all shone a bright, searing sun which seemed to be consuming us all.

8. Villegaignon

The admiral was unable to sleep.

He thought he had been awake all of the night, but surely that was not possible. He did not feel that tired, only hot and uncomfortable from the humid heat which enveloped the island, and totally awake with every fiber of his being.

It was often this way, and he knew from experience that there was no use trying to go back to sleep. His mind was already spinning. Better to get up and do something, put his mind to work at anything. Then, perhaps, sleep would return.

Tupí had no problem with insomnia. She was sound asleep in her little corner which she preferred to a civilized bed. Sound asleep, indeed; Villegaignon smiled. She was snoring softly, melodically, strangely. Perhaps one should not even categorize it as snoring. The sound did not irritate him, he who was irritated by so much in life.

He was so often astounded by this girl, this woman! She gentled him, made him, once in a while, into the kind of person he wished he could always be. We call them savages, he thought. She was cleaner than many a Frenchman and Frenchwoman on this island. She was loyal. She was happy. She was good to him. And for him. Villegaignon stood up from his bed and sighed.

He walked into his sitting room and decided it was too stuffy, although air flowed freely through the room. Glass was a luxury he would not afford and in this tropical land he was satisfied with openings instead of windows, with grillwork to keep out unwanted humans and animals, and wooden shutters to keep out inclement weather.

He wandered outside and stared at the starry sky. His eyes moved quickly to the Southern Cross, seen only south of the equator. It was a quiet and beautiful night.

The admiral wondered if he had been born under an unlucky star.

Things always seemed to go well for him, up to a point. And then there would be disaster. It was the story of his life!

That was what happened after he returned from his successful mission to Scotland. Mary of Guise, the lady of Lorraine, honored him. Henry the Second, king of France, made him vice admiral of Brittany. Villegaignon thought he would soon be invited to serve in the admiralty offices, serving His Majesty in his court.

And what happened?

He had been drinking too much and had an argument with a man who turned out to be the captain of the citadel at Brest. Reports were sent to Paris. Accusations were made about his manner of disciplining his men on the galleys and of his misuse of royal funds. Suddenly Henry was no longer a patron but a pursuer.

Had Coligny not interceded with Henry, Villegaignon would be in some prison, perhaps the Bastille!

But again his luck returned.

Almost by chance he had learned about plans to establish French outposts in the New World, including Brazil. He made his own plans with great care and detail. Gaspard Coligny, who was now head of the navy, thought them good enough to present to the king. Coligny also thought them good enough to mention to some of his Huguenot friends who were searching for new homes and opportunities.

His Majesty also approved of Villegaignon's plan to the extent that Henry provided two armed vessels and 10,000 francs for an expedition.

And he could take pride in what he had accomplished!

It was not a mean achievement to establish this much of an outpost of French civilization and military presence with so few people and resources. And many of his people in that first expedition had been recruited in provincial jails and prisons. Their motives for work were about as strong as their energies.

But here it stood. He gazed about him at the fortifications and the buildings. It was reality and one day France would honor him for this!

And, of course, the fact that he was now a wealthy man, or at least a wealthier man than he had once been, was not at all disagreeable. He owned four ships of his own with crews who were loyal and knew how to double and triple his investments. He chuckled at the implications of how his capital was growing.

Yes, his was a good life and held promise of becoming still better and more prosperous. If only he could believe it, he sighed. The return of these five Huguenots brought doubt and fear and literal pain. His stomach and bowels ached so he could not sleep when normal men slept.

Instinctively he spat toward Olaria across the bay.

How clearly he remembered that day in March, a year ago, when the second group of settlers had arrived. He had declared a holiday and there was a celebration. He was proud that so many people of skill and integrity had come. This was the way to establish a self-sufficient colony of France. A hundred new settlers, no less!

That was what he had thought, but even on the first day of their arrival he had his first premonition of trouble.

Jean Cointac came to see him as soon as it was possible to slip away from his fellow passengers without being seen.

"Welcome, monsieur!" Villegaignon had said, with a laugh. "I assume that is the proper form of address?"

"It is appropriate," Cointac smiled. They understood each other.

"Will you have some Calvados?"

"Yes indeed."

"It's excellent apple brandy from Normandy."

While they sipped their drinks, Villegaignon quickly perused the documents Cointac had brought. He set several papers aside for more careful reading later. He did take time to read a note from the Lord Chamberlain.

"You come with high recommendation, monsieur."

"Merci."

"How do you think you can assist me?"

"That is for your excellency to decide."

"You speak as a diplomat."

"I speak as a realist, excellency."

He smiled casually, it had seemed to the governor. Cointac

was clearly a man who knew his place and was comfortable with it.

"I asked the court for an adjutant," Villegaignon said. "This letter from the Lord Chamberlain does not make clear whether you have been sent as that person. It only says you have many competencies."

"I believe I have been sent for whatever use you can make of me. I have some experience in government. I have acquired some administrative skill. But you are the governor and you will make the decision how I can help."

"You speak with such precision. And without fear."

"I am beyond fear."

Cointac gave the impression of assurance and efficiency, as well as what many might interpret as arrogance. Perhaps that was what he meant by being a realist. The thought did cross the admiral's mind whether this young man had been sent to observe Villegaignon and report back to the court.

"Are you a lawyer?"

"I have studied the law."

"You avoid a direct answer. Are you a lawyer?"

"Excellency, I was a priest." Cointac smiled broadly.

Villegaignon was dumbfounded.

"Excellency, let me set your mind at ease. The Lord Chamberlain did write a fine letter of introduction. But that is all it is because the court is not certain of what I can do. I have no close ties with the court, believe me. I am here because of the intercession of a friend and some extraordinarily good luck. I committed no crime, but certain things did transpire which made my leaving France most desirable."

"You left with honor?"

"Yes, but I am an exile. A decision made voluntarily!"

"Are you still a priest?"

"One does not cease to be a priest."

"One can be excommunicated."

"But even so, a priest is not unconsecrated."

72

"Do you celebrate mass?"

"Not for many months."

"You have left the church, then?"

"Yes. And no."

"That is a strange answer."

"Man is mind and body and soul. Part of me left the church of Rome, part of me remains with her."

Villegaignon chuckled. "You must have had an interesting voyage. Did the Huguenots know you were a priest?"

"I do not think they did."

"Tell me about them."

"They are an interesting breed of people. Intelligent. Logical. All of them read and write, it seems. At least, they all seem to converse as university scholars!"

"Do you agree they are unemotional, cold, without humor?"

"Indeed not!" Cointac remonstrated. "Excellency, they are Frenchmen and no Frenchman is cold or unemotional. And French Huguenots feel very deeply about things."

Villegaignon laughed as he remembered the Huguenot capacity for outrage and anger. "Will there be problems for us?"

"Yes, I think there will be problems. These Huguenots take their faith quite seriously. There are two pastors. And they intend to be pastors and ministers. They held worship services twice a day and three times on Sunday aboard ship, and they'll want to establish something similar here on Coligny. They're planning for a celebration of the Holy Communion as soon as possible—the Lord's Supper, they call it."

"Nothing wrong with that, I don't suppose."

"Except that you will find them somewhat intolerant of other traditions and views."

"Isn't there a military man among them?"

"Yes. He is called du Pont. Be wary of him."

"Why?"

73

"He is a born leader but he has the good sense not to seek the center of attention. I don't think he will push himself into any position which you do not first offer to him. But he is a born leader and a competent military officer; he is a magnet and people flock to him."

"Should I offer him a position, do you think?"

"I think it would be wise. But I would be careful not to offer him too much, excellency. Make it a sort of gesture. There is another Huguenot with military experience, however, who might be of more immediate service to you."

"Who?"

"His name is Thoret. He fought in the Piedmont. He has experience in military matters. He is a practical man. And I think he will accept orders."

"Are you suggesting that du Pont would not accept orders?"

"We understand each other, monsieur."

"Cointac, have I made a mistake in bringing these Huguenots to this place?" It was a strange question for Villegaignon to ask for he was not accustomed to ask the opinion of others regarding actions he had taken. But he rather liked this cynical young man.

"Excellency, your reasons for inviting them are still valid. I predict difficult times, but we shall have to wait and see how you and they will get along!"

What a sly one he was! A more or less direct answer which committed him to nothing.

"May I venture a suggestion, excellency?"

"But of course," the admiral said.

"You may want to consider establishing some sort of council. These Huguenots are quite enamored by the notion of discussing issues carefully. It is their form of democracy. Like the ancient Greeks, these people like forums. They appreciate the opportunity of ventilating problems. It might be a way for you to govern more effectively and more easily."

"How large might such a council be?"

"The smaller the better I should think. Perhaps ten persons? Perhaps five representatives from the first immigration and five from this latest one."

"I like that."

"Not all need be Huguenots, obviously."

"It would be better if they were not."

"You would be the convener. The moderator."

"Cointac, I would be much more than that."

"Sir?"

"I would make all final decisions. I would carry them out. I am the governor, Cointac!"

"But of course, excellency."

The governor met with the two pastors the following day. Cointac was also present and this fact seemed to surprise the pastors.

"Monsieur Cointac serves as my scribe," the admiral explained. "He has had much experience in such matters and on this island I try to benefit from whatever skills the colonists bring!"

Villegaignon smiled warmly and the pastors readily accepted his explanation.

The admiral then went on to describe his plan for a colonial council. The pastors were delighted and said so.

"Now, let us discuss your own plans, reverend sir," the governor nodded toward Pastor Richier, "regarding the Holy Communion."

"First, excellency, there is no need to address me as reverend sir" Richier laughed. "Just call me pastor. That is what I hope to be, tending the flock God has entrusted to Brother Chartier and myself."

"Agreed, Pastor!" smiled Villegaignon.

"Secondly, we who are of the Reformed Faith refer to the sacrament as 'The Holy Supper' or 'The Last Supper.'"

"Pastor Richier, I do not concern myself with such hair-splittings." The admiral was still smiling. "I know you do not call it 'The Mass.'" The four men laughed briefly. "It is a Communion, is it not? And I am curious at this point as to which liturgy you will observe."

Both pastors seem bewildered.

"We have never commemorated or celebrated Communion in this place. Naturally, I am interested in the form it will take," Villegaignon continued.

The pastors still did not seem to understand.

"I think the admiral wishes to know which rite of worship you will follow," said Cointac, trying to be helpful. "The rite of Justin Martyr, Irineus, or Tertullian, for instance?"

"Excellency, if that is your question, then we will follow the practice, the rite established by our Lord, as sanctioned by Saint Paul, as followed by the church of the New Testament and our fellowship in the church at Geneva!" Pastor Richier smiled as he gave his reply but he seemed amazed that the question would be asked.

"I see," commented the admiral.

As he now paced the floor, these many months afterwards, he remembered that first Holy Supper all too well. It was there that he was publicly humiliated. And Cointac, also! He didn't care that much about Cointac being embarrassed but he did care about himself. The gall of that Huguenot expriest asking him if he confessed Jesus Christ as Lord! Later, the pastors had explained that it was necessary to make public confession of faith and that, once made, all were welcome to participate in Communion; that, in fact, true communion could never occur until such profession had been made.

The memory still rankled. He, a good *Catholic!* Well, perhaps not such a good Catholic—but at least publicly a Christian, governor of a Christian colony, asked publicly if he confessed Jesus Christ as Lord! It was absurd, it was insulting, it was unnecessary!

Fortunately, he had remembered enough of the Apostle's Creed to satisfy those stupid Huguenots.

Again he spat, this time powerfully, toward Olaria, where five of those heretics were probably sleeping, dreaming their dreams of treason.

And Villegaignon smiled. What they didn't know, of course, was that he knew.

He yawned. Gratefully the governor finally felt a drowsiness which might bring sleep.

9. La Fon

In my fever I continued to relive the horrors of the past months.

Two things happened which provided me with information I would not otherwise have received.

First, not to anyone's great surprise, I was appointed to be the admiral's personal tailor. Of course, I did try to be of service to the colony, but the admiral claimed most of my time and most of my work was done in his personal quarters.

While working in Villegaignon's house, I saw and heard many things.

Secondly, to everyone's surprise, or at least to my own, I was named to serve on the Council of government which had been newly formed. Ten of us were appointed, equally divided between the two immigrations. We were informed that the Council was to judge in matters of state and church. We learned within a few brief weeks that the Council might have opportunity to advise but it most assuredly had no power to judge anything. The governor was in charge of the Council at all times. And quite clearly, he was our judge.

It was only six weeks after we had arrived that I was finishing a uniform in the admiral's quarters when the two pastors arrived. Cointac was with Villegaignon. I was working in an adjacent room.

"I appreciate your coming so promptly," the admiral said in welcome.

"Will you take refreshment?" he asked.

The pastors indicated that they were satisfied.

"I called you to thank both of you for the superb manner in which you have begun your work here on Coligny," the admiral said, smiling broadly. "I note a change in the mood of the colony. And it is for the better!"

"Thank you, excellency," said Pastor Richier. His younger colleague, Chartier, remained silent. I was some distance away and, as I have already indicated, my eyesight is poor, and yet I thought that Chartier was puzzled by the manner and words of the governor.

"I have several questions to raise with you which I thought should best be presented privately," Villegaignon said.

"Excellency," questioned the younger minister, "by any chance are these questions which should be brought to the attention of the Council?"

"Perhaps, my young friend." Villegaignon seemed unperturbed and he continued to wear that strange, half-smile of his. "Frankly, I'm not sure we should trouble the Council with them. I have a few questions which I think are best asked by the governor to his two pastors. If we feel they need further discussion or explanation, we can decide that matter later!"

Chartier was very definitely puzzled.

"My questions refer to the observing of sacraments." There was ever so slight a change of tone in the admiral's voice, as if to say, the niceties are over and let's get down to business!

"Cointac, you will keep notes of our conversation."

"Yes, your excellency."

By now all of us knew that Cointac was a kind of personal secretary to the admiral. There were suggestions, also, that he was more than a scribe and that he was, in addition, an advisor of growing importance.

"My first question relates to marriage." Villegaignon directed the question to Pastor Richier.

"We were to be questioned about sacraments?"

"Yes."

"We of the Reformed faith do not regard marriage as a sacrament, excellency."

"How do you regard it?"

"As an institution ordained of God! I believe you know, sire, that we accept only two sacraments, namely baptism and the Lord's Supper."

"Very well. Let's still discuss marriage."

"If we can be of any service, excellency!" I was sure there was a twinkle in Richier's eye. I had heard him expound previously on how he would like to legitimize the admiral's relationship with the Indian girl, which was discussed much more widely than the admiral suspected.

"I am sure there are several who will want to be married, now that we have pastors to solemnize the nuptials." If the governor was aware of any personal implication in Richier's suggestion, he gave no indication.

"Chartier," the admiral continued, "I hear that you may soon decide to marry."

"The rumors are somewhat inaccurate," Chartier replied. His face reddened quickly but he was not one to mince words. "I had decided to marry long before I boarded your ship. The girl whom I shall marry, who has given me her promise, lives in Geneva."

"My felicitations, monsieur!" Villegaignon said, emphasizing *monsieur* in a stern voice. "You believe, sir, that it is proper for pastors to marry?"

"There is nothing in Scripture to forbid it, excellency!" Chartier affirmed.

"Priests do not marry!" said Villegaignon, crisply.

"May I speak to the question?" asked Richier.

"Proceed."

"Admiral, you speak of practices in the Roman church and overlook the fact that we are of the Reformed church. Reformed, excellency! The 'Changed Church,' if you will. We do not hold with the many additions which have occurred over the years, which were added without any sanction or basis in Scripture." Richier smiled. "I think it is amusing, excellency, that the Church of Rome says on the one hand that marriage is a sacrament and then, on the other hand, denies this great means of grace to its priests!"

It did not appear to me that Villegaignon nor Cointac were amused.

"Is it true that John Calvin is married?" the admiral asked.

"He is."

"And he is ordained?"

"I do not know," Pastor Richier replied.

His answer amazed me as I'm sure it amazed the admiral.

"What do you mean, you do not know?" he asked.

"As far as I know, John Calvin was never ordained as a priest."

"That is true," said Cointac.

"He studied theology at the Sorbonne but his major field of study was law, and he was a counselor, a lawyer."

"Was he not ordained a minister in the Genevan church?" asked Cointac, greatly intrigued.

"I do not know of it."

"He is just an ordinary Christian then!" Villegaignon exploded.

"There are no ordinary or extraordinary Christians, excellency," Richier said. "Some are doubtless better disciples than others but I subscribe to what Dr. Luther affirms, namely, the priesthood of all believers."

"Does Master Calvin participate in the Holy Communion?" the admiral asked.

"He participates weekly, if he is able."

"Does he distribute the elements?"

"Quite often. Of course, he is helped by William Farel at St. Peter's."

"If Calvin is unordained, by what right does he distribute the elements of Holy Communion?"

"By the same right that the early apostles and believers observed and shared the elements of this Holy Meal."

"I do not understand," said Villegaignon.

"Excellency, I am one who took holy orders, as you know," said Richier. "I am—or was—a Carmelite. And we have made much in the church of ordination and vows. The life of the early church, as recorded in Scripture, was much simpler. Fishermen were called and became disciples. At Pentecost they received God's Spirit in great power and they became leaders of the Church. That anointing of the Holy Spirit was of great import, but where do we read of their ordination?"

"And you affirm it is not necessary to be ordained to give the elements in Communion?"

"In a shared meal of remembrance, no, your excellency."

"Can a spiritual leader be effective if he is not ordained?"

"Excellency, was Jesus Christ Himself ordained?"

"He was a rabbi!"

"And a rabbi is a teacher. And Master Calvin is an excellent teacher and preacher. I wish you could hear him someday. At least, I hope you will have an opportunity, someday, to read his commentaries!"

"Let us talk instead about the Communion," said Villegaignon harshly. "I was surprised with many things you did at its celebration."

"We follow the custom of our Lord, of the early Church, and the Genevan Church," said Richier.

"Well, I think we can argue about what was the custom of the early church," said the admiral. "What can you tell us, Cointac? You have studied the matter!"

I did not think that Cointac relished the chance to participate in the discussion.

"The wine has not always been distributed to communicants," Cointac began, clearing his throat. "And from the record of earliest practices, wine was mixed with water, symbolizing the fact that when Christ's side was pierced, blood and water both flowed forth."

"Many strange and unscriptural customs developed over the centuries!" said Chartier, the younger pastor.

"Excellency, we can do nothing except follow Scripture," said Richier. "Our Lord left us a pattern, given to His disciples in the Upper Room. Bread and wine were distributed to all. We also have an order of service regarding the Lord's Supper given to us by Saint Paul, who also writes about sharing both bread and wine—and nowhere is anything said about mixing water with wine."

The admiral stared at Pastor Richier.

"Continue!" he said.

"The Meal of Remembrance, the Lord's Supper, is not a complicated thing. Why should we make it so? The Meal is for all believers. Why should we limit it?"

"This is all very strange to me," said the admiral.

"Excellency, with all respect, you have not attended a Reformed service of worship, have you?" asked Chartier.

"Only here, since you arrived."

"Then, in time, perhaps you will become accustomed to our ways!" Chartier said, with considerable enthusiasm.

"Perhaps his excellency does not wish to become accustomed to our ways," Richier said to his colleague, suggesting by the tone of his voice, I thought, that his youthful co-worker be more cautious in his comments.

"And what do you mean by that, Richier?" asked Villegaignon.

"Excellency, I am not aware that you have indicated any desire to become a Huguenot. And I am not aware that any of us has tried to influence you in that direction."

"I have said, publicly, that I will defend your rights with my person and with my wealth!"

"We appreciate that commitment, excellency."

"But it is true that I have not declared myself a Huguenot."

"Excellency, are you still a member of the Church of Rome?"

The admiral's face turned red and I knew he was angry.

"You are beginning to interrogate me."

"I apologize, excellency."

"All you need to remember, both you Richier and you Chartier, is that I am the governor, the representative of His Catholic Majesty, Henry!"

"But, sire," Richier injected, "you did invite us to come and you did make certain promises to us regarding the freedom we would enjoy to worship as our conscience convinced us."

Villegaignon remained silent.

"And excellency," Richier continued, "if our form of worship offends you or displeases you, surely you are free to invite other persons as you see fit. Summon a priest, a Lutheran, or even an Anabaptist if you like."

"You play games with me, Genevan!" Villegaignon was livid. "We will speak about this at another time." He stood up, turned his back on the pastors and Cointac, and left the room.

The matter came up briefly at the next meeting of our Council.

We discussed many matters and I suppose we spent no more than five minutes with the issue of Holy Communion.

It was agreed by the Council, without dissent, that Communion be held once a month. The Genevan pastors would have preferred a weekly observance but did not insist upon their view being adopted.

The Council was dismissed. Villegaignon, however, asked the pastors to remain. Cointac, of course, was also present. The pastors later relayed to us what transpired.

Villegaignon presented a document to the Genevans.

"This document relates to the matter of observances of Holy Baptism and Communion in this colony," he began. "Be so good as to review it."

The ministers were stunned.

"Excellency, this appears to be a statute!" Richier said.

"It is."

"But this has not come before the Council!" Chartier pleaded.

"True," said the admiral. "This statute deals with details which are of no concern to the Council."

The pastors looked at each other in disbelief.

"First, in regard to baptism. This rite shall be observed by using salt, oil, and saliva."

"Excellency, are you jesting with us?" asked Richier.

"I am as serious as I can be," the admiral replied.

"I have never heard of such a rite!" said Richier.

"It is the rite of Saint Clement," said the admiral. "Surely you have heard of it, surely you know it!"

"I know of baptism being symbolized only with the use of water, excellency," said Richier.

"These other things are absurdities, sire!" Chartier exclaimed.

"The practice of the early church fathers are not to be characterized as absurdities, sir!" said Villegaignon coldly.

"Now, to matters of the Holy Communion," he continued. "No longer will it be required to have persons make public professions of their faith." He glowered at Richier, who told me about it later. "Since the bread becomes holy after the words of consecration, a piece of it should be preserved as a holy relic. Further, wine shall be mixed with water."

"Excellency, I cannot believe what I hear!" Richier exclaimed. "You cannot force a specific order of worship upon us! You cannot!"

"But I am doing so, Richier."

"The Council has not voted upon this, sire!" Chartier interposed. "The Council was established to judge matters of state and church."

"This matter is inappropriate for the Council," said Villegaignon.

"Were the Council to pass such a decree, excellency," said Richier, "I would still consider it inappropriate. And not binding upon my person!"

"You agreed to the Council's decision regarding monthly observance of the Sacrament."

"That, sire, did not involve a question of conviction."

"But this is now to be our procedure, our statute!" said Villegaignon.

"I will not consider it binding upon myself," said Richier.

"Nor I!" agreed Chartier.

"You would defy me?" asked the admiral.

"Excellency," Richier sighed, "we were promised freedom to worship as Huguenots. Now you decree that we may not worship as Huguenots. In fact, you would require me to function again as a priest of the Roman Church, which I cannot, in conscience, do."

"Sire, forgive me, but I feel you are confused," said Chartier. "You cannot expect ministers of the church of Geneva to accept this statute. It is contrary to Scripture. It is contrary to the reform we believe God wills for His Church."

"Some say the Reformers are heretics."

"Excellency, you said you would defend the church of Geneva with your life and your wealth."

"This is a colony of France, not Geneva!" Villegaignon shouted.

"And monsieur Villegaignon," said Richier softly, "the Genevan Reformation is truly a French Reformation. John Calvin was born in Noyon. William Farel is from Auvergne. Both emigrated to Geneva. Both studied at the Sorbonne under Lefevre, whose translation of the Bible into French we read here in our services! The reform movement is not foreign to France, excellency. Far from it!"

"I have come to one conclusion, monsieurs," Villegaignon said. "And that is that I believe the early church fathers must be closer to the truth than our present-day Reformers. Surely you must admit that they lived closer to the actual time of Christ and the apostles. Surely they were more aware of how the early church conducted its affairs. It is that state of conduct and practice to which I would have us return."

"It is a return to Rome—or are you establishing your own form of reform?" asked Richier.

Villegaignon did not answer but smiled mysteriously, cryptically.

"We praise God for the Fathers of the Church," said Pastor Richier, "and we praise Him still more for Holy Scripture. We stand upon it, excellency. As with Dr. Luther, we can do no other!"

"You have been deceived, sire!" Chartier said suddenly,

pointing his finger at Cointac.

The admiral walked quickly to the young preacher and slapped his face with his right hand.

"I make up my own mind, Guillaume Chartier!" he said in a harsh whisper.

"I do not care what I said heretofore," Villegaignon continued, in a loud voice. "This statute is the law in this small part of France! It will be observed!"

"Excellency, I am an old man and I am tired," Richier sighed. "Do with me what you like. I see no purpose in argument. But I promise you that I will never adhere to your statute!"

We experienced another strange event the following day.

It involved Thoret and La Faucille.

Thoret, a Huguenot, had been appointed adjutant for military affairs on the island; du Pont had been offered the position but for his own reasons had declined Villegaignon's offer.

La Faucille was the admiral's steward in charge of the port, having responsibility for unloading and loading ships, accounting for supplies and seeing that they were properly stored. La Faucille was a man of good intentions but limited abilities.

The two men saw each other frequently and often worked together. Usually they got along splendidly. One day, however, they had an argument and came to blows.

La Faucille was overseeing some work at the wharf, where a ship was being unloaded by several Indians. They were not working as hard as they could as La Faucille saw it, and, cursing them soundly, he had them whipped.

Thoret did not approve of such behavior—neither the cursing nor the whipping. He said as much to La Faucille, calling him aside so that the Indians would not hear what he had to say.

They began to argue about jurisdiction and prerogatives.

Perhaps the day was overly humid or they were tired. At any rate they began to fight and challenged each other to a duel.

The matter was brought before our Council.

We had passed a rule that when a public fight occurred, the guilty party, as determined by the Council, would kneel in front of the offended party for a period of one-half hour. We thought this was a more humane solution to this kind of problem. It was certainly preferable to a public flogging and we thought it would discourage further altercations and, perhaps, bloodshed.

When Thoret and La Faucille appeared before our Council, both had cooled off, had apologized to each other, and felt foolish about the entire affair. They were even willing to forego questions of personal honor and wanted to forget the challenge to a duel.

We heard both of them speak to the matter and we agreed as a Council to declare both men guilty, to suspend the prescribed penalty, and merely give each person a gentle reprimand.

The admiral, however, thought otherwise. And since he was judge, as well as presiding officer, his will prevailed.

"Thoret initiated the abuse and he is guilty," he said. "We cannot begin to make exceptions. He must be punished in the manner established by the Council!"

Thoret was furious and had to be restrained. I think he would have attacked Villegaignon.

"Patience, brother," said Pastor Richier, who was there. "It is a bad decision but accept it as a good soldier of Jesus Christ."

La Faucille was one of the original colonists and to some of us it seemed that the admiral had taken sides against the newcomers and, more specifically, against the Huguenots. But there was nothing the Council could do. The admiral was governor, prosecutor, and judge.

As things turned out, our Council would hold only one

more session before it would be disbanded.

Thoret carried out his sentence. He knelt publicly, in front of La Faucille, in the square at the center of the fort. He knelt for a half hour, in the blazing sun. La Faucille had the grace, at least, to be embarrassed by it.

And our admiral felt obliged to add to Thoret's insult. He stripped Thoret of his command and gave it to La Faucille, who then became adjutant as well as port steward. Thoret was assigned to routine construction work.

Things grew intolerable for Huguenots. Now that the admiral's feelings and prejudices were known to everyone, many of the older settlers, who cared nothing for morality and Christian behavior, openly began to taunt every Huguenot they met. Their language was vile and sometimes obscene. There was occasional physical abuse as well and we grew more fearful for our families and our future.

Thoret had had his fill and one day he disappeared from the island. Villegaignon ordered a thorough search but he was nowhere on the island. Thoret, we learned subsequently, had built a raft of scrap lumber and logs during his spare moments and had sailed toward the mainland. There were rumors that he was a stowaway on a ship headed for France, other rumors claimed that he made some sort of arrangement with a friendly captain. Anyway, he was not to be found in Olaria and, as far as we knew, he was not hiding on the mainland. There was no question where our sympathies lay. We hoped and prayed that Thoret had been successful in his escape.

A final insult was given to Pastor Richier one Friday afternoon. The admiral commanded him to appear in his quarters and handed him another document.

"I have prepared a list of topics I wish to have you discuss in your sermons," said Villegaignon without preamble.

"Has it now come to this?" asked Richier. "Are you now telling me what I should preach about?"

"That is a safe assumption, pastor."

"I wish I were your pastor," Richier said wryly.

The following Sunday, Richier preached a sermon we would long remember.

He began by showing the list of sermon topics he had been given the preceding Friday. Villegaignon was seated in the congregation.

"The Word of God will not be bound!" declared Pastor Richier.

"Man has tried in countless ways to bind the Word of God, to write his own substitute word. He has done this by enacting laws, by declaring edicts of the church, by relying upon tradition instead of Scripture. I have been told how baptism and the Lord's Supper are to be observed. Now I have been told what to preach! But, my friends, not even his excellency, the governor, can shackle Holy Scripture! And I shall preach the Word which God's Spirit leads me to preach!"

Pastor Richier then slowly tore the list of sermon topics into little pieces.

Villegaignon was on his feet.

"You go too far, Richier!" he shouted. "Let me debate with you!"

"Admiral, there is a time and place for debate. In the council chamber!" He did not go on to point out that the Council had by now been dissolved. "This is a service of divine worship and not a forum for disputation!"

The admiral was sputtering something which I could not hear.

"Let us sing triumphantly the hymn of Master Calvin!" shouted Richier over the uproar.

And we sang the hymn loudly and lustily.

> I greet Thee, who my sure Redeemer art,
> My only trust and Saviour of my heart,
> Who pain didst undergo for my poor sake;
> I pray Thee from our hearts all cares to take.

The admiral charged out of the congregation. We continued to sing the entire hymn. Its final verse, to me, seemed especially significant.

> Our hope is in no other save in Thee,
> Our faith is built upon Thy promise free;
> Lord, give us peace, and make us calm and sure,
> That in Thy strength we evermore endure.

Villegaignon never again returned to our Huguenot service of worship. Three weeks later, a new decree no longer allowed us to conduct public worship. We could meet privately, but only once a week, and only by ourselves. The penalty was also proscribed that any Huguenot conducting public worship would be imprisoned for twenty days and given only bread and water, and any person attending such public worship would be flogged with twenty lashes.

The next time we worshipped, privately, following the admiral's directive, Pastor Richier requested that we remain following the benediction.

"Our situation here grows worse, as we all know," he began. "The time has come to evaluate our situation and decide what we shall do. I have asked monsieur du Pont to moderate."

Philippe du Pont stood up and came forward. He was a tall, distinguished-looking, and very intelligent man. I thought to myself, *This is the man who should be governor of this colony!*

"It is clear that we have been gravely deceived in our coming to this new land," he began. "As we all know, we subscribed our names to an agreement to remain here for at least two years."

"Villegaignon has broken that agreement!" Bourdel exploded. "He promised freedom of worship, among other things. Whatever remains of the agreement is invalid!"

"Bourdel is right!" many of us shouted.

"We should overthrow the tyrant!" Jacques Balleur was shaking his fist in anger.

"That is a possible response," said du Pont softly. "I would caution my brother not to raise his voice in raising the possibility. If this is a direction we should explore, we must speak carefully, cautiously, and quietly. We are surrounded by our enemies."

Balleur sat down.

"Is rebellion, open rebellion, an appropriate action for us to take?" du Pont asked our group.

We began to discuss the question animatedly.

"Please, one at a time! Share your thoughts with everyone!" du Pont said.

"Rebellion should be a last resort!" I said.

"There was a mutiny here before we arrived," said Pastor Richier. "It was suppressed. Successfully suppressed."

"We are outnumbered two to one," Bourdon commented.

"Perhaps the best thing we can do is to return to France," I said.

"How will we go?" asked Jacques. "Villegaignon's ships won't take us."

"There are other ships," said Bourdel. "There are ships which do not fly Villegaignon's coat of arms. There are these private vessels."

"There are few such ships," said Richier.

"But they do arrive from time to time," said Bourdel.

"And how will we pay for passage?" asked Jacques Balleur.

"We can sell what we have. We can combine what money we now have. It is worth a try!" I said.

And that is what we decided, finally. We agreed not to rebel but, rather, to leave the colony quickly and quietly.

We sold whatever we could to other colonists, both on the island and to settlers living on the mainland in Olaria. We sold odd pieces of clothing, cloth, cooking utensils, tools, even a few items of jewelry. One of the settlers on the main-

93

land traded with the Indians and sold a few items to them.

Through him, we made our own contact with an Indian tribe and traded a few trinkets and clothing items we still had for two casks of peppercorn, which had high value in France. This we considered to be an investment to give us some money when we returned.

After we had sold everything we could and counted the money we had earned and still had within our possession, we found we had something like one hundred escudos. An escudo was a Spanish gold piece, and common currency in the New World.

An old, decrepit caravelle called the *Jacques* arrived one day. Its captain took pity upon us and agreed to take some passengers.

After appropriate haggling, it was agreed that only sixteen of us could go and the cost would be exactly one hundred escudos. There were some fifty Huguenots, including children, on the island; and the decision as to who would be numbered among the fortunate sixteen was a difficult one.

We petitioned for permission to leave, since there existed the agreement regarding our employment at Coligny. Also, the captain of the *Jacques* required a license to sail and transport cargo from Coligny.

Villegaignon delayed for several days, raising objections or remaining in seclusion, refusing to see anyone or answer any questions.

Then, suddenly and unexpectedly, he called the entire colony together.

"The time has come to say farewell!" he shouted. He was angry and red-faced and barely in control of himself. "You Huguenots are the refuse of the earth. Not once have you given me a good day's work. Always you have argued. Always you have debated. Always you have been insolent."

He shook his fist at us.

"You have my permission to go! Go to France or go to

hell. Just never return to Coligny!"

He turned without another word or gesture, returning to his quarters.

I knew then that Villegaignon was not only a cruel man. I knew then that he was also a miserable and very sick man.

10. Villegaignon

Sleep still eluded the admiral. A cooling breeze now made the early morning hours more pleasant, but the approaching dawn erased the visibility of the stars.

He had sensed these changes as he dozed and would waken intermittently as images of faces and events crossed his mind.

Villegaignon finally accepted the fact that there would be no more sleep this night, and he opened his eyes.

The last image to cross his mind had been that of Cointac.

Despite the deterioration of affairs, he had liked the young man. To be sure, much of him remained a mystery. But Cointac was a man of intellect, talent, and much information. He was urbane and useful.

He had turned to him on the day that Carmelite, Richier, had defied him. The preacher announced he would not abide by the admiral's decree regarding baptism and communion.

"Cointac, I would welcome your advice," he had said. "What should we do about these Huguenots?"

"Nothing."

"What do you mean? We must do something!" Villegaignon insisted.

"The affair is beyond solution or reconciliation, your Grace," Cointac had said.

"They must be convinced of the rightness of my position!"

"And that is of supreme importance to you, sire." Cointac sighed.

"These Reformed Genevans will not listen to anything but Scripture or Calvin!" Villegaignon said.

"And if you press them, excellency, I think you will find that they will defer to Scripture rather than to Calvin."

"I need these colonists, Cointac. They are good people and good workers. Can anything be done?" The admiral considered relenting.

"I have one suggestion," said Cointac, "but it will take some courage to accept."

"Let me hear it."

"Draw up a list of questions regarding faith and practice of faith. Tell the Huguenot leaders that these are questions which concern you and that you feel you need additional counsel to answer or resolve them."

"Where would I obtain such help? I won't ask the Genevans for their advice!"

"I think you should submit your questions to the universities of Wittenberg, Geneva, and Paris. Ask the theologians there to respond to your questions. Promise to formulate your decision on what you learn from these authorities."

"Why should I consider those three universities?"

"Because it would be readily accepted by all parties concerned. You go to Paris because of the Sorbonne; a French governor would surely want to do this. You should include Geneva simply because this is the source of Huguenot conviction and understanding. You ought to include Wittenberg, in my view, because anyone concerned about the reformation of the Church must give serious consideration to the Lutherans."

"Perhaps that would settle the controversy," Villegaignon mused. "I still would not appreciate public debate on these issues."

"You could prohibit public worship but allow the Huguenots to worship privately and not enforce your directive regarding the sacraments until answers are received to your questions."

"Your suggestion has merit. Who would go?"

"How about Chartier?"

"The young pastor. Yes, that is good," said Villegaignon. "He is a firebrand and it would be better if he were some distance from Coligny." He thought for a moment. "We will do it!"

And it had been arranged. The questions were formulated, the Huguenots agreed to them and to the procedure, and plans were made to send Pastor Chartier as the bearer of questions. Two of the admiral's ships were in port, soon to return to France, and Chartier and a small party would travel on them. Cointac made copies of the questions. Villegaignon wrote the letter which would accompany them; he had insisted upon doing this himself.

Within the hour after they had sailed, Cointac was at his door, obviously disturbed and troubled.

"I must see you, excellency!" he said.

"But of course, Cointac. I am at your service," Villegaignon had replied.

"They have sailed."

"Yes, I know. Is there a problem?"

"Yes, I believe there may be several problems."

"Sit down, Cointac."

"I would prefer to stand, excellency."

The admiral simply could not understand what had come over his adjutant. Cointac was belligerent, no question about that!

"First, excellency, it is my understanding that you had Chartier placed on one ship and his five companions on the other."

"That is true."

"Why, admiral? Why?"

"Because I chose to issue the order."

"I'm sorry, excellency, but that is not a sufficient reason for me."

"I'm not sure I owe you any explanation, Cointac!" Villegaignon was beginning to bristle.

"That is true, sire. But an explanation would be helpful."

"I did not wish Chartier to confer and plot with his colleagues."

"Excellency, they will have a journey of, perhaps, twelve weeks or more! It is cruel to separate them! They committed no crime!"

"It has been done. But surely this is not what upsets you."

"There is something else. Far more serious!"

"Proceed."

"I have learned that you sent the communication with the list of questions only to the Sorbonne."

"Yes."

"Again I must ask why."

"And again I see no reason why I should answer to you, Cointac!"

"In this instance I believe you do owe me an explanation. The idea of the inquiry was mine. I spent hours copying the questions for the three universities. We had an agreement with the Huguenots. I felt that I was a party to that understanding. Now, I am made to feel as though I am a liar."

"The decision was mine."

"And the Huguenots are furious!"

"It appears to me that you are, too."

"Yes, I am."

"Cointac, I do not choose to become further involved with the heretics in Germany or Geneva. I will abide by what the authorities in Paris have to say."

"We know already how those authorities will answer," said Cointac. "The radicals, the reformers have been expelled from the theological faculty. The authorities who are there are biased in favor of Rome and tradition."

"Yes."

"Why engage in this kind of charade, excellency? Why spend the time and money for a foregone conclusion?"

"Because I require the imprimatur of authority."

"I thought you were interested in ascertaining opinion, to learn truth."

"I will not trouble myself further with truth."

Cointac slammed his fist into his hand.

"It is impossible. I cannot believe that it has come to this!"

"Cointac, do not be so disturbed!"

"Chartier will not return. I would not, if I were in his place! Better to remain in Europe."

"I do not expect him to return. He has a girl friend in Geneva, remember? He won't come back. He'll stay on to marry!"

"You planned it this way!"

"Now I only have the old man, the Carmelite, to deal with."

"Of what value is your word, sire?"

"Careful, Cointac."

"I have been careful for too long, excellency. I have tried to understand you, to serve you, to defend you. I came to your defense countless times." He sighed. "But no more, sire. I have no faith left in your word, in your agreements, and in your person."

"You speak treason!"

"I speak the truth."

"Get out of here!" Villegainon shouted.

"With pleasure, monsieur." Villegaignon remembered that Cointac's face was white and he appeared to be close to fainting; but he stood erect and firm. "I never signed an agreement with you, thank God. I came in response to your special appeal to the court."

"But you are not an emissary of the court!"

"No."

"You said you had to leave France."

"I have my reasons for being here, yes. And I do not have powerful friends in the Palace to whom I could report the things which transpire in this place." He walked toward the door. "I wish to God that I did."

"Cointac, you cannot leave! I will not allow it!"

"Not allow it?" Cointac laughed. "Excellency, I no longer work for you."

"At least tell me your plans."

"Sir, I do not intend to tell you my plans." Cointac looked directly and intently into Villegaignon's eyes. "I do not say this lightly. But may God help you, admiral, for you truly need help."

Cointac had disappeared that very night. As with Thoret, he seemed to vanish from the face of the earth. Unlike the situation with Thoret, there was no raft and no caravelle was anchored in the bay.

His leaving was a very great pity, mused Villegaignon. He had thought Cointac to have the mettle and strength of himself. He had misjudged the man.

But he had not misjudged these five Huguenots who had returned. The admiral had drawn up another list of theological questions and La Faucille, his military aid, would carry them to Olaria.

The end of this miserable impasse was in sight. Villegaignon smiled. He not only was fully awake but fully alive. It would be a good day. He knew it! And he would waken the girl to tell her.

11. La Fon

Despite my age, it now appeared that I might be more fortunate than Pierre Bourdon.

My fever had broken and, again, I was able to take solid food. Pierre, on the other hand, continued to fight his fever and could tolerate only occasional cups of broth, fish chowder, or tea. He was growing weaker and we truly feared for his life.

Bourdel was worried and preoccupied. He had expected

an immediate response from the admiral—and it was neither immediate nor, when it came, what we had expected.

All of us wanted to work. I know I looked forward to doing something physical, something with my hands. I was never one who enjoyed being sick.

The other three, whom the fever had overlooked, found things to do in Olaria. Mostly they helped people who needed an extra hand, or something to be mended. It was something to occupy their time, they said. The people paid them with what they could spare. That meant food, usually. Very little money could be spared.

Earning some money became quite important to us as we pondered our future. We would have to buy our way back to the homeland.

During this time of waiting we began to recount our memories. Jean de Lery wrote them down meticulously in his journals. He firmly believed that the power of his pen would one day be a means of bringing Villegaignon to justice.

We were chatting with Lery that evening, after supper. We were in a rather joyous mood, considering our circumstances. I think we were especially happy that Pierre was able to sit up briefly and seemed to be feeling better than he had in days.

We suddenly heard the clapping of hands outside, indicating that someone wished to see us.

It was La Faucille, the admiral's adjutant for the fortress.

He seemed to be nervous and embarrassed. As far as I was concerned, he would never be the commandant that Thoret had been. But that was Villegaignon's problem, not mine.

"Welcome, La Faucille," said Bourdel.

"May I come in?" he asked.

"Please enter."

"You are managing well I trust?" he said after finding a place to sit.

"We have been ill and hungry," said Matthieu.

"Your rèturn has been a great surprise."

"It came as something of a surprise to us, too!" I said. Jacques laughed at my jest.

"I am here on official business," La Faucille said. "I have a communication from the governor."

"We have been hoping to hear from him!" said Bourdel, beaming with delight.

La Faucille seemed to be amazed at what Bourdel had just said.

"We must find some sort of employment you see," Bourdel continued. "And the admiral promised each of us a job."

"Ah, that is what you had in mind!" La Faucille sighed.

"You do bring word of this?" asked Bourdel.

"Yes," the adjutant said, again growing nervous. "There is work for you. You can return to the island tomorrow, if you like."

"Wonderful!" Bourdel exclaimed.

"However, I bring you this document, monsieur Bourdel," La Faucille said. "It must be read and its provisions carried out before you can return to the island and resume your work."

"This is a strange thing to require," Bourdel said.

"This document contains several questions to which Admiral Nicholas de Villegaignon demands response by tomorrow morning." La Faucille had obviously rehearsed his little speech many times and was glad it was over."

"I do not understand why we must answer anything!"

"The governor explained to me that these are basically the questions he sent with Pastor Chartier to France. Since no answers have yet been received and since the questions still concern the faith and practices of Huguenots, he simply wants to know how you respond to these questions before he again extends the hospitality of the fortress to Huguenots."

"Hospitality?" I whispered to Jacques. He winked back at me.

"We are to do this in less than twelve hours?" asked Bourdel.

"Yes," said La Faucille.

"It will be necessary to work through the night."

"I fully suspect that will be so, monsieur."

"The admiral said nothing about questions when he talked to us!"

"You will find everything in order in this document," said La Faucille, "just as the governor wrote it."

"It is senseless and irrational!" Jacques declared.

"I assure you that this is not a frivolous order," the adjutant said. "The governor is most adamant." He paused and sighed; I was sure he did not enjoy his assignment. "I shall return tomorrow. In the morning. For now, bon soir."

Jean Bourdel read the list of questions to us.

"Do you accept the Trinity?"

"What is your understanding of the Blessed Sacrament?"

"Why do you not mix water with the sacramental wine?"

"Do you pray for the dead?"

There were seventeen questions in all. They sounded familiar because they had been raised before.

"This is no mere inqiury!" Lery exclaimed. "The admiral wants you to compose a confession of faith!"

"And I say it is a trick," said Jacques le Balleur.

"How do you know, Jacques?" asked Bourdel.

"I do not trust that overstuffed swine."

"Apparently he will keep his word regarding work."

"But why does he require this confession?"

"As he said, there has been controversy with the Huguenots. He wants to know where we stand."

"He knows full well where we stand."

"He ought to."

"Then tell me why we must answer these questions?"

"Because the admiral insists," Bourdel said softly. "That is an important consideration."

"You are absolutely blind when it comes to trusting that animal."

"I do not trust him, Jacques. My trust is more highly placed than that! But I think I know what we must do. Furthermore, we have one more opportunity to defend our faith, to witness to our belief in Jesus Christ. Surely that is nothing we should fear."

"I wonder," sighed Jacques. "But you already know how I feel about returning to the island to work. And I see no purpose in answering his questions. Let the scholars at the Sorbonne—or wherever—do that."

We heard a strange cough at the doorway and turned.

"Cointac!" I shouted.

"May I enter?" he asked.

"But, of course!" I said.

Jean Cointac had never been a husky man, but he had lost considerable weight. He no longer looked like the clever and debonair secretary to Villegaignon we had once known. He now wore an untrimmed beard. His eyes were sunken into their sockets. His clothes were clean and bleached by the sun, but they were torn in several places. He wore no shoes.

"You are hungry," I said as I handed him some bread and went to prepare him a cup of hot tea.

"Thank you," he said as he took the bread. "You are surprised to see me?"

"That does not overstate the matter," Bourdel said with a grin.

"And I suspect that you do not trust me," Cointac continued.

"You were working for the admiral, Cointac!" Jacques said.

"I understand your apprehension," Cointac agreed. "I was

advisor to Villegaignon. Or so it was thought." He smiled. "No one advises the admiral, ultimately. You need not fear me. Please believe that! I have nothing more to do with Villegaignon."

"But after so long an absence, you suddenly appear!" Bourdel exclaimed.

"And it was only within the hour that La Faucille was here," I added.

"Is that not a strange coincidence, Cointac?" asked Jacques.

"What can I say?" Cointac replied. "It is a coincidence."

"Where have you lived, Cointac? How have you lived?" asked Lery.

"My wife and I live in the south, several leagues from here."

"That's right. You were married just before your disappearance," I recalled.

"I married the girl from Rouen."

"The one you met aboard ship!" I smiled. "Good." As I have mentioned before, I have fond memories of Rouen from when my Mathilde and I had been there. I thought of Mathilde more often now and certainly with no less of a sense of loss.

"You live with the Portuguese?" Bourdel asked.

"Yes. They have a large settlement at São Vicente, Saint Vincent."

"That is where you live?"

"No. There are newer settlements. Much closer to here. The Portuguese are moving northward, all along the escarpment."

"How do the Portuguese tolerate a Frenchman?"

"I speak some Portuguese. And I have tried to give the impression that I am a Basque, or at least a French-speaking Basque!"

"And you have managed?"

"It has been possible to live. There is food, not a great deal, but enough. And the Portuguese are not so bad."

He accepted more bread and some fruit.

"Are you alone, here?"

"I am."

"How does your wife fare, living with the Portuguese?" I asked.

"It is possible to exist," Cointac said, with profound sadness I thought.

"She was a very pretty girl," I said. "I remember her from the voyage. You are happy?"

"Yes."

"You know, many of us thought you were a Roman priest," I laughed. "And we gossiped much about you and the girl."

"I still believe you are, or were, a priest," said Bourdel, without a trace of a smile.

"You guessed correctly, Bourdel," said Cointac. "I was a priest. I had a parish near Lyons. But I gave it up."

"What are you then?"

"In my beliefs?"

"Yes."

"It is easier to say what I am not, rather than what I am." Cointac shook his head slowly. "Can you understand that?"

"Perhaps," said Bourdel.

"Do you know the name Jacobus Faber Stapulensis?"

"Of course! Except we know him better as Jacques Lefevre, our brother in Christ who translated the Holy Scriptures into French!"

"The Sorbonne condemned his writings, but I read two of his books. I also met the man."

"You did!" Bourdel exclaimed. "How I would have liked to have conversed with him."

"I saw him at the chateau at Blois, where he taught the royal children for a time. Anyway, I think Lefevre set me on a

110

course from which I could not retreat."

"Lefevre influenced many other men," said Bourdel. "John Calvin, for one. Although that was many long years ago."

"But what do you now consider yourself, Cointac?" I asked.

"I no longer serve the Church of Rome. And I am not a Lutheran. Nor am I a Huguenot. You see, it is easier for me to say what I am not."

"A man who thinks is something," said Bourdel. "Surely you are a believer."

"I consider myself a Christian," Cointac affirmed. "A seeking Christian. A dissatisfied Christian."

"Then we have much in common," Bourdel smiled.

"I suppose I thought that in some way Villegaignon would find another pathway," Cointac sighed. "Something neither Roman nor Reformed."

"This may be what the admiral is attempting to do," said Lery.

"But if that is the case, it is not the way I choose to travel," Cointac said.

Jacques took a step toward our visitor.

"Monsieur Cointac, why are you here?" he asked. "We have already asked that question and I do not believe you have answered it."

"I heard that Frenchmen had returned in a small boat. I was curious, I suppose. I wanted to learn what had happened."

"You heard of our return? How is that possible?" asked Bourdel.

"The Indians travel widely and they are bearers of news."

"Surely it is dangerous for you here."

"I have no doubt that the admiral would kill me if he found me. I shall not give him that pleasure."

"I cannot believe you came so far just to learn which

Huguenots returned!" said Jacques. "I'm sorry, Cointac, but there has to be a greater reason."

"And you are still suspicious."

"I do not trust the admiral. And I'm not sure I yet trust the man who once sat and stood at his right hand."

"Very well, I will tell you the truth." Cointac declared, "I was hunting some two days' distance from Olaria. I met some Indians who told me of the return of five Frenchmen in a small boat. I was curious about you, and I am curious about other matters here. Perhaps I became a bit nostalgic. I don't have many friends, but I have two or three here in Olaria. And I have not heard French spoken in three months, except for speaking it with my wife. I felt I was close enough to chance a visit at night. I have another visit or two to make. And then I shall be gone, before morning, before Villegaignon can receive any word of my presence."

Jacques scratched his head.

"I cannot force you to believe me, monsieur," Cointac said, "but I tell you the truth."

"And why did you wish to see us?" asked Bourdel. "That still puzzles me, inasmuch as we were not the closest of comrades!"

"I wanted to hear your story. I abandoned the admiral when I learned that he had broken his word."

"About sending the questions?"

"Yes. He had agreed to my suggestion to send them to Paris, Geneva, and Wittenberg. And when Chartier sailed, his orders were to submit the questions only to the Sorbonne. Yes, the rumors of that were true! That is when I left. And, of course, Richier and the rest of you were still on the island. So tell me what happened."

Bourdel summarized the events of harrassment on the island, our coming to Olaria, our sailing, and our disaster which forced our return.

112

"And the admiral has been in touch with you?" asked Cointac.

"He visited us at this very place!" I said.

"He has promised us work," said Bourdel.

"And I am trying to convince my brothers not to return to the island under any circumstances!" shouted Jacques.

Cointac nodded his head affirmatively.

Bourdel looked at each of us.

"Do I have your permission to share this document with monsieur Cointac?" he asked.

There was no objection.

"This is the document La Faucille brought to us, earlier this evening." Bourdel handed the list of questions to Cointac. "We are to give an answer, at the admiral's command, before we are allowed to return to work on the island."

"How much time is given you to prepare your response?"

"We have until the morning."

"Twelve hours or less?" Cointac said with amazement. "Absurd!"

He quickly read through the list of seventeen questions. He shook his head in disbelief.

"Surely you don't intend to answer him?"

"Bourdel wants to answer him!" Jacques exclaimed.

"You should not humor that madman."

"Do we have a choice, I wonder?" asked Bourdel.

"You can escape. You can leave this place. Go anywhere, while there is still time!"

"Why should we escape, Cointac?" asked Bourdel coldly. "Do you know something more? Have you learned something we should know?"

"I only know that he hates you. Perhaps he is possessed of a demon. But he is an evil man and I would not return to the island, and I would not for a minute cater to his fancy of being some sort of a theologian by answering these questions."

"Cointac, that is precisely what I have been telling Bourdel for the past hour!" said Jacques. "Bourdel, listen to Cointac!"

"You know his cruelty," Cointac continued. "You know his word is without value."

"Where can five of us escape, Cointac?" Bourdel exclaimed. "It's easy for you. You're only one person!"

"The forests can accommodate several times our number. You can come with me!"

"And join the Portuguese?" I asked.

"There are many more ships arriving at Saint Vincent than here. There is work to be had."

"But we are Frenchmen," I said. "And we don't speak Portuguese as you do. We would be arrested."

"There may be a greater chance for survival with the Portuguese than here, my friends."

"You say there are ships in your port, Cointac," said Bourdel. "But none of them would carry us to France. I doubt whether Frenchmen, like ourselves, would even be taken to Portugal unless it would be as prisoners."

He began to pace the floor.

"Each one of our party is free to do as he wishes. But I want everyone to understand that I want the opportunity to return to my homeland as a free man! I don't want to be a prisoner of the Portuguese, nor of an Indian tribe."

"By remaining, you are likely to be a prisoner of Villegaignon!" said Jacques.

"It is a risk." Bourdel sighed, then pulling himself up straight with a firm voice said, "and to write this confession requested by the admiral is an obligation. It is also an opportunity. It may be God's way of opening the admiral's eyes!"

"You have much to discuss and to decide," said Cointac, rising, and excusing himself. "I am pleased we were again able to meet. God speed!"

"Go in peace, Cointac," said Bourdel.

Cointac slipped out quickly and silently.

We ourselves were silent for several moments, reflecting upon our two visits that evening.

"I feel sorry for Cointac," I said, finally breaking the mood.

"I once thought he was a spy for Rome," said Bourdel. "He may now be a spy for Portugal."

"Do you think that is why he came to Olaria?" I asked. That possibility had not entered my mind.

"Who knows?" Bourdel sighed. "I hope he is still loyal enough to his country not to bring her harm. I suspect the Portuguese, if they are moving northward, would like to know how fortifications may have been strengthened, how many ships may be in our port, that sort of thing."

"He may have been forced to come," I said. "Perhaps they hold his wife as a hostage."

"You have a vivid imagination!" Lery chuckled.

"And if what you say is true," said Jacques harshly, "he won't gather much traitorous information during the night."

"You are right, Jacques," said Bourdel.

"And he is right about Villegaignon!" he shouted.

"The time has come to decide," said Bourdel. "Not only whether to stay or escape, but, if we stay, do we answer these questions of the admiral."

Matthieu Verneuil had been quiet all evening. He was very pale. I wondered if he were getting the fever. Pierre Bourdon was still quite ill, although he was awake and in the room with us.

"I will stay!" said Matthieu. "I don't know about the Portuguese, but I know I don't want to become an Indian. And let's begin to write the confession!"

"Pierre, have you been listening?" asked Bourdel.

He closed his eyes and moved his head up and down.

"How do you vote?" Bourdel continued. "Do we stay?"

Again he nodded affirmatively.

"And I will stay," I said. "Who else will take care of Pierre?"

"And the document?"

"Let's give Villegaignon a good answer!" I said. "We've been through all of this before, several times! Let's take our stand, come what may!" Frankly, I was getting impatient and I felt we would have much work to do that night.

We all looked at Jacques.

"I will go with Cointac," he said. "I believe you should, too, to salvage what we can of life and faith."

"Jacques, my comrade, go with God!" said Bourdel. "Cointac is a new ally. Perhaps a good one. But God is better!" Then he grabbed Jacques' shoulders, pulling him in an embrace. All of us, except Pierre, did likewise. Pierre raised a feeble hand and Jacques grasped it. I confess that our eyes were moist and we could not speak for a time.

"My things are ready," Jacques said. "Such as they are. I think I shall try to find Cointac tonight, so we'll be ready to leave before dawn. Perhaps we shall meet again."

"Perhaps not on earth, Jacques," said Bourdel. "But we shall meet again."

12. La Fon

There was no sleep for us that night. Even Pierre, who continued to fight his fever, was awake and amazingly alert.

Jean Bourdel reviewed the seventeen questions in the admiral's document.

"It would take a month to properly respond!" said Matthieu Vernueil.

But we had less than half a day. Only the few hours which remained of the night.

"It isn't all that bad," said Bourdel. "The questions overlap. There are really only seven or eight areas to consider."

"Eight or seventeen? What difference, Jean!" Matthieu exclaimed. "There isn't enough time."

"There is time," Bourdel whispered calmly. I was glad that he was a schoolmaster. He knew what to do with such an assignment, how to begin.

"The first question is about our belief in God, whether we are truly Trinitarians," he said. "There is a question about the last judgment. Then several on the Lord's Supper."

"Let's be careful with our answers to those," I said. "They're likely the most important questions as far as Villegaignon is concerned."

Bourdel agreed with me with a quick nod. "Then there's an inquiry about free will."

"Something with which to bait the Calvinists," said Matthieu.

We laughed.

"And there are other questions about absolution, marriage, ordination, sacred orders, and prayers for the dead."

"And that is all?" asked Matthieu with considerable sarcasm.

"It is sufficient," Bourdel answered. "Now, how do we proceed?"

"I think you should proceed, Jean," I said. "You are the best educated. You know how to answer these things."

Pierre nodded agreement from his pallet.

"And I also agree," said Matthieu. "Write what you think is the best answer, then read each item back to us. We'll argue with you if we don't agree."

"Very well," said Bourdel. "I only wish I had some of the books Pastor Richier took back with him."

"We have a copy of the Holy Scriptures," I said. "That should be enough. Let us refer to the Bible for our answers."

"It ought to be enough, as you put it, André," Bourdel

said. "Villegaignon, however, is so impressed with what the early church fathers had to say about this and that. I believe they would agree with many of our positions. It would be helpful to refer to them, also," he sighed.

Matthieu stood up. "Bourdel, you don't have to write a book!" he said. "There isn't time for that—or any long-winded debates!"

"I agree!" I said. Bourdel was a good man but he could make mountains out of molehills, building them with words.

"You are both telling me not to be a schoolmaster," he chuckled.

"I think a schoolmaster can write a very good reply," I said, "but I think it should be simple and brief."

"And, Jean, we must begin!" said Matthieu.

We took only a few minutes to agree upon the first answer, the first article of our creed.

> We believe in one God, immortal and invisible, creator of heaven and earth, creator of all things visible and invisible, who is distinct in three persons: the Father, the Son, and the Holy Spirit; who, nevertheless, are of one substance, in an eternal essence; who are also of one will. We believe in the Father, the fountain and beginning of all good; in the Son, eternally generated by the Father, who, in the fullness of time, made himself known to the world in the flesh, conceived by the Holy Spirit, born of the Virgin Mary, made under the law to rescue those who lived under the law, so that we might be adopted as proper sons ourselves; and we believe in the Holy Spirit, proceeding from the Father and the Son, teacher of all truth, who spoke through the mouths of the prophets, and who inspired all things said by our Lord Jesus Christ and the Apostles. The Holy Spirit is our comforter in affliction, who keeps us steadfast, and helps us to persevere in all that is good.

As Bourdel read it through a final time, I thought it was a formidable beginning to our answer. Perhaps it is similar to other statements of faith. We did try to remember what we could of the ancient creeds, and we wanted to state clearly only what we believed.

It took us much longer to decide on how to answer the questions about the Lord's Supper, or the Blessed Sacrament, as the admiral put it.

"Do you think Villegaignon has returned to Rome?" asked Matthieu. "In his faith, I mean."

"Why do you ask that?" said Bourdel.

"Because if he has, the answers to these questions should cause us much difficulty."

"We don't know that he has again espoused the Roman Catholic faith." I said. "Only a few months ago he made a public profession of faith in a Huguenot service."

"And much has happened since then," said Bourdel.

"And much has happened in France, if the rumors are true," Matthieu said. "I heard things at the wharf. Stories about intrigues and plots in the court. Huguenots are not as acceptable as they once were."

"What has this to do with us?" asked Bourdel.

"Nothing, I suppose," said Matthieu. "Except that we must be careful about what we say."

"We must be truthful, Matthieu, not careful!" I said. "Although I agree that we must be sure of what we answer—and not only what we answer in regard to Holy Communion."

"He asks how we understand the Blessed Sacrament, what occurs at the consecration of the elements," Bourdel reminded us. "I think it is important that we state clearly that we believe the bread and wine to be symbols only. That way we avoid the interpretation of transubstantiation or even Luther's doctrine of consubstantiation."

I shook my head. "Those words mean nothing to me, Jean."

"They mean a great deal to the admiral."

"Always we come back to the fact that Christ himself said

121

'This is my body!' " Matthieu said. "We can't get away from those words."

"They were symbolic words," answered Bourdel, "as we have heard so many times. Christ used real wine and real bread. As symbols!"

"But he said 'This is my body!' "

"In another place he said, 'I am the door!' Did he mean he himself was a literal door? He many times spoke in symbols."

"That is a good point," Matthieu agreed. "But let's not irritate the admiral with a reference to it."

"There are some references from St. Augustine which I do remember and could include," said Bourdel. "In essence, he said that the Lord's Supper is a spiritual meal, that it is food for our souls and not food for our bodies, and we should not make more of it than that."

"Villegaignon would say that is exactly what he believes: that bread and wine literally become the body and blood of Christ, something spiritual!"

"He would be wrong," said Bourdel. "I think he believes in a literal transformation; there's nothing spiritual about that. It's a different matter entirely to partake symbolically of bread and wine and allow God's spirit to transform this into a spiritual food for our souls."

I shook my head in consternation.

"André," he said to me, "the important thing is to remember Jesus Christ. Not to be distracted by so many other things, so much dogma, an insistence that so many other things are happening. It ought to be so very simple! Common wine, common bread. To remind us of Jesus in a special way."

"I get very confused," I said. "I cannot understand why such a simple act must create so much debate! The Church of Rome calls it the Mass."

"And they mean by it a sacrificial meal, literally!" Bourdel interrupted.

122

"And others call it the Eucharist, Holy Communion, the Blessed Sacrament, the Lord's Supper, the Holy Meal," I continued. "What difference does it make, really? Why can't we remember Christ in our own way, and the admiral in his?"

"Isn't part of our controversy the fact that we wish to remember Christ in our own way?"

"And you would allow the admiral to do likewise?"

"I have no quarrel if the admiral wishes to understand the sacrament in his own particular way."

"Then what is at issue, Jean?" I pleaded. "Is it so terribly important that we not mix the wine with water, for example?"

"That, André, is a side issue. The quarrel we have is that Villegaignon insists that we observe the Lord's Supper in his way, and only in his way."

"I'm not sure that it matters that much, really, if we partake of the Holy Meal in his way," I persisted. "The admiral, for whatever reasons he may have, insists upon a certain form and a certain liturgy. Can't we simply go along with him and still believe as we have, as Reformed Christians?"

"I can only speak for myself," said Bourdel, with a trace of anger, "but this is now a matter of integrity and belief. It is not just a matter of practice. We are asked, now, to state how we view the matter, what we believe! I cannot tell the admiral what he should believe but I must witness to my own faith, without compromise!"

Bourdel stood up and began to pace the floor.

"To accept the admiral's position would mean that certain specific words must be said over the bread and wine and spoken by specific persons. In his view, because of that incantation, a miracle takes place. The admiral insisted that our Reformed ministers say those precise words in a precise way, wearing prescribed vestments, using approved holy vessels. And because Villegaignon believes that the transformation, the miracle, truly occurs—that the bread is truly Christ's flesh, that the wine is truly Christ's blood—all communicant Christians must somehow worship this bread—elevate it, bow down to it, preserve it, because now it is truly part of Christ! And as for the wine, the blood, we cannot share it with common Christians, nor can it be preserved. Rather, only the priest can partake of it, all of it. And it goes on and on."

He loomed over the table with great intensity. "I believe we must worship God with our minds as well as with our souls. I cannot intellectually accept the belief of the admiral. I believe the bread continues in its nature and substance to be bread, just as the wine remains wine, without change or alteration. This does not mean that the bread and wine are necessarily common; they are dedicated to a special use. I believe this is logical. I believe this is in keeping with the teaching of Scripture. I believe this was the practice of the early Church. I believe this is the way I can best remember Jesus Christ until He comes again!" He pounded the table. "And this is what I must bear witness to!"

"And I believe that this must be written!" said Matthieu.

"We are the Church Reformed according to the Word of God," Bourdel said. "Not the Church according to the Church Fathers, nor according to traditions, nor according to Villegaignon's interpretation of these."

I had closed my eyes, not in sleep, but in thought.

"You disagree with me, André?" Bourdon asked.

"I agree with your stand, but I wish the Lord's table did not divide Christians," I sighed. "It ought to be the one place where we can be together and adore our Lord without argument and rancor."

"You are correct," he said. "But each of us must answer for himself. The admiral will answer to God, as will I. As will each of us. I simply want to be free to worship God as I believe He is to be worshipped. And I am still a free man to the extent that I can write down what I believe!"

We agreed, finally, on what should be said in regard to the observance of the Lord's Supper.

This was the way it went throughout the night. Jean Bourdel would discuss, we would react, he would write, and then read, and again we would react, and often Bourdel would write some more.

Pierre had fallen asleep. Matthieu and I dozed but Bourdel would awaken us to ask for an opinion or approval.

As dawn was breaking, the document was finished. We called Jean de Lery, as he had requested, to make a copy of the confession for the collection of writings and memoirs he was making. And then we awakened Pierre so that we might read through the entire document, article by article. One or two changes were made, and Lery made the same changes on his copy.

It was a good statement and we were proud of Jean Bourdel and his magnificent job accomplished in so brief a time. We were silent for a time, sensing a presence beyond ourselves as well as this moment of supreme significance for ourselves and for our brothers and sisters in the faith.

And then we each signed the document. Bourdel first, then Verneuil, then Pierre, to whom we brought the document where he lay. My signature, that of André La Fon, was last.

The confession was ready for the admiral to read.* La Faucille could come for it whenever he wished.

*Note: The entire confession, as copied by Jean de Lery and later printed by Jean Crespin, appears at the close of this book.

13. La Fon

La Faucille arrived as he had promised, in the early part of the morning, approximately twelve hours after he had left us the preceding night.

He was surprised that we had completed the task.

"I wasn't sure you would write the statement," he said, looking at the manuscript. "You must have stayed up the entire night."

"We did," said Bourdel.

"And now you can take it to your master, Faucille," Matthieu taunted, "with our compliments."

La Faucille started to say something but decided against it.

"I thank you, gentlemen," he said with a shrug of his shoulders.

"When will we receive word about returning to the island for work?" asked Bourdel.

"I do not know," said La Faucille. "That is up to the governor. Perhaps later today."

He stood in our doorway, a rather forlorn and despondent figure, a man chosen to be chief officer of the fort. He had had no ambition, nor ability in my view, for the task. "Good day," he said, with great sadness.

All of us were tired but try as we would, it was difficult to sleep. The day was warm and humid and most uncomfortable. The air hovered as though it were lead and we all felt its weight upon us. You must remember that this day in February was a summer day in this land south of the equator.

The day was a Thursday. The date was February 8.

Strange as it sounds, in spite of the almost suffocating heat we seemed at times to be numbed by a chill. Perhaps it was preoccupation or apprehension or even fear. Perhaps this was due merely to our exhaustion, both physical and emotional.

Since we could not sleep, we busied ourselves as best we could. I gathered some sticks and pieces of wood outside for our cooking fire. Bourdel decided to go to town to the shore to fish and, perhaps, pick up some news. Lery decided to wash a few clothes. Matthieu picked up a broken stool and began to repair it.

As I returned with fuel for our fire, Pierre Bourdon motioned to me and I went immediately to where he was lying.

"How are you today, Pierre?" I asked. I felt his forehead and he was still running a fever, but it seemed to me that

127

perhaps it was not as severe as heretofore.

"I feel better, André!" he said with a trace of a smile. "I am so weak, though!"

"Of course you are weak," I said. "You have had a fever for twelve days. You haven't eaten. You've lost weight. And you'd better not exhaust yourself."

"I'd like to talk to you, André. I haven't been able to talk to anyone for a long time."

"I'm glad you want to talk, but don't overdo it!"

"I wish I were able to help Matthieu with that broken stool."

"You'd do a faster job of it," I laughed. "He's better with ironware than with lumber."

"André, what is going to happen?"

"We expect that we'll soon be going to the island to work."

"I wonder."

"You have doubts?"

"I am afraid, André."

"And so am I," I sighed. "In spite of everything. Perhaps we should not have written that confession. Who are we, really? A tailor, a turner, a blacksmith, a schoolteacher."

"We had to make our public profession, André," Pierre said. "We could not have lived with ourselves if we had refused to do so. We did the right thing. I agreed with everything, even though I could only nod once in a while!"

"Nevertheless, you are afraid."

"I fear I shall never again see Marie."

"Your wife. So that is it."

"There is much you do not know, André."

"I know what it is like for a young man to miss being with his wife. I speak to you as I would to my son, who is married, and whom I have not seen in so many months. I was young once. And I was married once!"

"I kept dreaming about her in my fever. But I could never reach her, I could never touch her!"

128

"You were very happy, weren't you!"

"We were. But we argued the night before we left the *Jacques.*"

"Young people often argue. I know that, too."

"But I remember the sadness in her eyes when we left in the long boat. André, I never asked her forgiveness!"

"I see." Suddenly I understood what overwhelmed this young man who had been the strongest of our group.

"I wonder if God has punished me with this fever for what I failed to do!"

"God does not punish in that way!" I affirmed. "Why don't you tell me what happened," I suggested, knowing that Pierre had to talk out his fear and worry with someone, that this had probably plagued him as much as his fever during the past several days.

"Marie is pregnant."

"Wonderful!" I exclaimed.

"She has carried the child for five months." He paused. "I am ashamed of myself. On that crowded ship, that night before we left, I wanted very much to be—" He sighed. "To be very close to my wife."

I nodded that I understood. And I did.

"She wasn't feeling well and she had been seasick during the day. And she has always been shy. And that night she rebuffed me with an anger I had never seen in her before." It was hard for Pierre to speak about these matters because he also was shy. "I too became angry. And I did not sleep beside her that night."

"And the five of us left the next day."

"André, I really decided to go with you because I felt that it was the right thing to do!"

I tried to smile.

"But I know Marie felt that I left in my anger. That was why she was so sad. If only I had spoken to her, explained to her, asked her forgiveness!"

"Easy, now!" I said. "Your fever will return and where will you be?"

"I should never have left her."

"Perhaps, Pierre. But she is halfway to France now."

"You do think so?"

"I am sure of it. And there is nothing you can do about your decision now. You are here and she is there. If your love for each other is strong enough, just as you now feel remorse, so will Marie. And she has probably already forgiven you, castigating herself, blaming herself for turning you away and provoking you."

"She should not do that; it was my fault entirely!"

"Ah, but you forget that it is the nature of women to be tender and forgiving."

"I hope you are right. When we embraced, I only said farewell!"

"If it please God, one day you will be together again. And all this will be forgotten. For now, you can pray to God and ask his forgiveness if you haven't yet done so, and ask him to care for Marie and your child in his special way."

"La Fon, you are a good man. You have given me absolution."

"You made your confession," I smiled. "Now rest for a while."

"I will," he said. His face was flushed but happier now, and he closed his eyes and it seemed to me that his lips were moving slowly in prayer.

Bourdel returned with a fish, quite a good-sized one, and I prepared the coals. We would not try to keep this fish until supper; the weather was too warm and the fish would spoil.

We ate inside where it was somewhat cooler. In spite of the heat, we had one of the most joyous meals we had shared in many a day. There was laughing and joking, as if the tensions of the past week and night had suddenly evaporated.

"There is still time for you to escape!" said Lery, trying to make a serious point.

"Lery," I shouted, "I am tired of the subject!"

"We made our decision yesterday," said Matthieu. "We stay, no matter what happens!"

"Lery, enjoy your fish!" said Bourdel. "Everything will be fine. We'll soon be going to the island to work. We'll save our money together and in three or four months we'll be ready to board a ship for home!"

"And if there isn't work on the island," I said, "I'm going to go from house to house here in Olaria with my needle and thread and resume my profession as tailor." The others laughed.

"Matthieu," said Bourdel, "did you know that somebody is trying to set up a blacksmith's shop in town?"

"Good! I'll have to look in."

"Somebody found a forge someplace."

"And if worse becomes the worst, then I shall go out and pick peppercorns in the jungle," laughed Bourdel. "There's no need to trade with anyone. We can find the spices ourselves."

"Bourdel," I said, "perhaps we can also trade. Get some of those beautiful stones the Indians carry from the mountains!"

"We don't even need the admiral and his poor jobs on the island!" shouted Matthieu. Even Pierre was smiling broadly.

I think we all knew better but for a few moments we indulged in our fantasies.

"La Fon, what will be the first thing you will do when you return to France?" asked Bourdel.

"I have thought of that day many, many times," I said. "It will not be one thing, but several things. First I shall drink a large cold glass of milk. Then I shall eat a dish of soft cheese. And then I shall have a slice of warm, freshly-baked bread, covered with butter."

"Be quiet!" shouted Matthieu, good-naturedly. "Dairy products!"

"You speak as a true Norman, André," said Bourdel.

"Where else in the world is there such dairy cattle?" I asked.

"Certainly not in Brazil!" said Matthieu.

Pierre had raised himself on one arm and was laughing.

"What will be the first thing you will do in France, Pierre?" asked Bourdel.

"That may be an embarrassing question!" I teased.

"I will go directly to wherever my Marie is!" Pierre said.

"By then he will probably be a father!" I announced.

We paused for congratulations.

"And what will you do, Bourdel?" I asked, after the felicitations to Pierre had subsided.

"I want to visit a bookstore and see all of the new books which have been printed. I want to attend a Reformed service of worship—but I should like to go to Geneva and to Saint Peter's for that! And then, I should just like to walk and watch people, hear their chatter and their laughter. It would not matter whether I did that in Geneva, Lyons, or Paris."

"Lery, are you going to stay here for the rest of your life?" Matthieu inquired.

"I have decided to return to France, as soon as I can arrange my affairs. Perhaps we shall sail together! And I can tell you the first thing I plan to do. I shall go to Paris and to the office of the admiralty, and there I shall lodge a formal complaint against Admiral Villegaignon. This is why I have been collecting all of these documents and recording all of these events. I shall never be satisfied until justice is done and this governor is called to account for his tyranny!"

Our conversation continued throughout the afternoon. We mused, we dreamed. We had taken our stand in regard to our faith. We thought we saw the beginning of a new freedom, that soon we would have another chance to return to our homes. Ours was a mood of expectation and hope and joy. Of course we were poor and without resources, but we felt the presence of our God, we had our friendship with each other, and just talking about better days in the future made this particular day one to remember.

They arrived that same day, on Thursday, just before sundown. There were ten of them, sailors and guards from the island, and all were armed. They surrounded our hut.

Their leader was a man I knew as Raoul. There were rumors to the effect that he was a convicted murderer. He had been one of the original colonists. Perhaps one should not trust appearances and impressions, but Raoul was a huge man physically and he certainly looked like a ruffian.

"I seek four men," he said. "Jean du Bourdel, Matthieu Verneuil, Pierre Bourdon, and André La Fon." This was odd, for he knew us all.

"I am Bourdel, as you very well know. You have brought word from the admiral?"

Raoul called four men to join him.

"Who is that man?" Raoul asked, pointing to Pierre.

"Pierre Bourdon. He is seriously ill."

"We leave him here with a guard until the morning."

"There is no need for a guard!" said Bourdel.

Raoul did not answer. "There are five of you here. I seek only four." This strange interrogation seemed unreal.

"I am Jean de Lery. I have lived here for six months and this is my place."

"We have no interest in you, Lery. At least, not at the present time," Raoul said with a sneer.

"May I ask what is your intention?" Bourdel inquired. The guards had now surrounded us.

"You are under arrest. By order of the governor."

"For what reason?" exploded Bourdel.

"You are the four who signed the confession?"

"We are."

"Then you are the four persons to be arrested."

"For what reason, Raoul?" I shouted.

"Have patience, La Fon!" he teased. "You will know the charges before the stars appear."

"Lery, we have been betrayed!" Bourdel said sadly.

"Silence!" commanded Raoul.

"Take care of Pierre."

"He will join you tomorrow," the chief guard said as he began to prod us. "Now, on to the boat!"

14. La Fon

We were marched from the jail to the admiral's quarters.

He was seated behind a table, wearing a white uniform I had made for him several months before. We were not invited to sit down.

"Where is Jacques le Balleur?" he demanded.

"He is no longer with us," answered Bourdel.

"I have eyes, I can see that!" Villegaignon cried out impatiently. "But you have not answered my question. Where is he?"

"In truth, I cannot say, excellency," said Bourdel. "He decided to leave us and he was a free man to do so."

He has joined your exiles, I thought to myself. I was pleased with Bourdel's answer. It was true. And surely this was no time to volunteer additional information. I hoped that Jacques and Cointac were many leagues from here.

"He was not with you when this confession was signed?" the admiral asked, waving the document before us.

"No, sire."

"And do you four verify that you did sign this document?"

We moved forward.

"Have a good look. Are these your signatures?"

The confession was ours, as were the signatures.

"I think you lie about Balleur," the admiral said. "He is probably hiding in the forest outside Olaria."

"We have no reason to lie, excellency!" I said.

"Silence, tailor!" he shouted at me. "What would you know about it? Except that all of you are spies who have come back to make havoc in this colony."

"Spies?" Bourdel exclaimed. And then he laughed. "Is it possible that your excellency truly believes that of us?"

"You have yet to deny it."

"We have no desire nor strength for intrigue or spying. We wish only to be left alone, to earn some money, and to return to our homes. This is what we hoped to do once before until we had to leave the ship so others could complete their voyage."

"That ship of yours is only two days' distance from here."

We looked at each other in amazement. Perhaps the admiral had received some intelligence, some information of which we were unaware.

"Sire, the *Jacques* should be halfway to France!" said Bourdel. "At least I hope that it is. Pierre's wife is aboard that ship. And other women and children. We pray daily for the ship's safety."

"I do not believe you."

"Excellency, there isn't enough food and water on that vessel for her to be anchored somewhere near here. We left because of the short supply!"

"You have sent Balleur to get word to the ship."

It was absurd. I was about to blurt out that Balleur was with his former counselor, but I bit my lip instead.

"Say nothing!" whispered Bourdon. "Nothing!"

Villegaignon stood and walked to where we stood, sitting on the edge of the table.

"Say nothing, La Fon!" he mimicked. "The conspiracy is so obvious. And, Bourdel, you never fooled me for a moment."

"There was no conspiracy, sire."

"Your return and your alleged disaster were too obvious, too contrived. Clever, to be sure, but as false as your assertion that you do not know where your colleague is." He paused. "I know that he is with Cointac."

Our faces fell and I am sure we gave the appearance of being guilty.

"I have my own spies, you see. And I also know that Cointac is a traitor. I know he has been living with the Portuguese. And perhaps he has arranged for a Portuguese warship to sail northward to join Richier in an attack upon me."

"Sire, while we did not tell you about Cointac, it is true that we do not know where either of them are at this moment."

"I have strengthened the garrison and we shall repulse any attack which may come. And you will not be rescued, messieurs. Your plan has failed."

"We had no such plan, admiral," said Bourdel. "But am I to understand that we are to be kept imprisoned until the *"Jacques* returns?"

"Now, why should I do that, Bourdel?" sneered Villegaignon. "I have had my own plan. And you have followed it beautifully."

"Why have we been arrested?" asked Bourdel. "Because

you think we are spies?"

"The reason is on that table!" beamed the admiral, pointing to our confession.

"Sire, you requested that we answer certain questions! We merely followed your orders."

"And you have convicted yourselves."

"Of what, excellency?"

"Of heresy."

Matthieu had been quiet up to this point but now he exploded. "First we are accused of being spies, and now of being heretics! I demand that we be brought before the Council! I demand we be tried legally as citizens of France!"

"There is no Council, Verneuil," said the governor, "or have you forgotten!"

"It should be reconvened!"

"There is no Council," Villegaignon said with finality. "There is only me. I am His Majesty's representative. I have the proper patents. I have the authority to maintain order on this distant piece of France. You are enemies of that order and I can no longer allow you to freely disseminate the kind of treason with which you have soiled the paper upon which your confession is written."

"It is not treason!" shouted Bourdel. "It is a statement of belief!"

"It does not represent the holy Catholic faith of our sovereign."

"King Henry allows freedom of worship to Huguenots. You also promised it to us when we agreed to join your colony. We never pretended to be other than Huguenots, so obviously our confession is not one of the Holy Catholic faith, as you put it!"

"Times change, Bourdel," said the admiral. "And people change."

"But you made promises!"

"The promises to Huguenots are not being kept in France.

There is a growing reaction to the Reform. Henry won't be king forever and when Francis is king, his queen will be Mary Stuart, whom I knew as a little girl, whose mother I served for a time in Scotland."

"You professed yourself to be a Huguenot only eight months ago. That you would defend this faith with your person and your wealth!"

"And that was before you Huguenots publicly humiliated me."

He waved the confession in our faces.

"Now, answer me carefully," he said. "Does this confession reflect your beliefs in regard to the questions I raised with you?"

We agreed that it did.

"Is there anything you would change?"

We did not answer.

"Then you stand together on this document?"

We glanced at each other and saw that we were still in agreement. We nodded to Bourdel to speak for us.

"Excellency, we spent the night composing this confession. We are quite familiar with it now, having read it to each other several times. We do stand on it. We can do nothing else."

Villegaignon stood away from the table, facing Bourdel.

"You quote much Scripture, which does not surprise me," he said. "But in several places you quote the church Fathers, particularly Saint Augustine."

"Yes."

"I would like you to document those quotations."

"That would be most difficult, excellency. I do not have access to a library."

"In what book, in what place does Augustine affirm, for example, that the elements of the Holy Sacrament are only a sign of Christ's body?"

"I just know that he said it, that he wrote it. I have heard it mentioned by ministers of the Gospel many times."

"But I only have your word."

"Sire, I have a memory for such things. I may not have every word correctly, but I have written the true sense of what these early Fathers wrote!"

"You lie!" Villegaignon struck Bourdel across the cheek with his fat, heavy hand. The mighty blow drew blood from his mouth.

There were tears in Bourdel's eyes, but he said nothing. He stood erect, not moving a muscle.

"You are crying, Bourdel!" sneered Villegaignon. "Finally we have our mixture of blood and water. Let me add to it!" And he spat in Bourdel's face. "You woman!"

I felt Matthieu ready to lunge at the admiral and grabbed his hand, holding him back. He understood my meaning, and we all remained silent in the face of this insanity.

"Gardien!" Villegaignon shouted. The jailer appeared quickly. He must have been standing outside the door and I suspect he heard and saw everything which had transpired.

"Take these Huguenot heretics back to their cells. Give them no food or drink. And if any should decide to renounce their adherence to this foolish confession of theirs, they may send word to me through you."

The admiral then turned to Bourdel, whose face no longer was bleeding. The cut was only a superficial one.

"I promise you this, Bourdel," the admiral hissed in anger. "I know you are the leader of this group and I promise you that I will not taste food until I receive satisfaction for your obstinacy." They glared at each other. Then the admiral shouted, turning his back upon us, "Take them away!"

It was still Thursday, close to midnight.

There was no moon as we walked through the dark night, feeling our way carefully along the pathway back to the jail and our cells. We were placed in separate cells so that we could not communicate with each other. That, too, was an order of the admiral, we learned.

There were stars to be seen in this black night, however. Through the window of my cell I again saw the Southern Cross, a configuration we never saw in France, which seemed to beam with a special and unusual brilliance. Perhaps its light would bring some hope to our heavy and troubled hearts.

15. Villegaignon

Dawn would be here within two hours. Raoul was now in
Olaria. La Faucille and Gardien were standing before the
admiral in his quarters.

"Is there no other way, excellency?" asked the commandant.

The admiral shook his head. "There is no other way." He
felt strangely cold. He also felt a nagging, gnawing pain in his
lower guts, which made him nauseous. That particular pain

had been recurring; he breathed deeply and felt the spasm pass.

"Is everything in readiness?" he asked.

His garrison commander and his jailer nodded.

"Gardien, no one spoke to you during the night? No one wished to reconsider, to retract, to speak with me?"

"No one, excellency. There was some singing."

"Singing? At a time like this?"

"They are strange people. They sing their psalms, lustily."

Villegaignon pushed several papers across the table.

"I require your signatures on these documents."

Faucille looked at them nervously.

"Sign them!" shouted the admiral. "You are witnesses to my report of high crimes committed at the colony of Coligny. The report is in order. It only requires your names."

The two cohorts added their signatures. Gardien wrote with great difficulty.

"Quickly, Gardien!" urged the governor. "These papers will be carried to France and will go to the archives. We observe the legalities."

Soon the sentences listed in his report would be carried out. Villegaignon reflected that never before had he written a report about something to take place in the future. Nothing had better go wrong. But nothing would.

"Go to your posts and await me. You know the time."

Both men grunted their knowledge. They left quietly and quickly.

If only Jacques Balleur had not disappeared, thought Villegaignon. That presented many problems. It convinced the admiral that the Huguenot vessel was only a few leagues away, that a careful plot to attack and overthrow him was in motion.

And now he had to move quickly to complete his own plan. He had to do this before people in this fort were awake. He had to finish the job before Balleur made contact with the ship, before his fortress would come under attack. He would rise to this occasion as he had to so many others.

But it would be a long dreary day. The admiral was quite certain of that.

16. La Fon

We were awakened just before dawn by Gardien, the jailer. This particular Friday, February 9, 1558, began quietly with a slowly rising mist.

"What happens now, Gardien?" I asked. "Another meeting with the governor?"

"I have nothing to say!" he said, turning his face from me brusquely.

"Look, Gardien," I said, "don't treat an old friend this way!

We are from the same part of France. You were the first colonist I met here on the island. You were my first friend!"

"You had best forget about our being friends." He coughed nervously and would not look me directly in the eye.

"Why are we suddenly no longer friends?" I inquired.

"Forget it!"

"Why?"

"Because it's now too dangerous, that's why!" he whispered intently.

"Surely you don't believe that foolishness about our being spies! Do I look like a spy! I am a tailor, nothing more!"

"You should never have written that confession."

"Is that what makes it dangerous to be friends?"

"You have given the admiral everything he wants. You should have escaped to the forest, run off somewhere! But, like fools, you had to return to the island."

I was beginning to agree with him. We should not have asked to return to the fortress for work. I wasn't sure whether we should have written the confession; that was a matter of conscience and conviction. But I was quite sure now that nothing we had written would ever convince the admiral of the rightness of our belief.

"Gardien, I am still your friend," I said.

He looked at me in surprised amazement, adjusted my leg shackles, and escorted me to where Bourdel and Verneuil were standing.

"Good morning," I greeted them. In spite of the lack of sleep during the preceding two days, I felt remarkably good.

"Courage, André!" whispered Verneuil.

"We shall soon be free!" Bourdel added.

They were calm but unsmiling.

"Get moving!" shouted Gardien.

The Scottish guards accompanied us, each carrying a sack of something I could not identify in the hazy half-light of the morning. Two persons walked some distance ahead of us. They were only silhouettes but I was sure that one was Villegaignon; no one else on the island possessed his girth. The other person was likely La Faucille.

Our leg shackles made walking slow and difficult, and the clanging of the chains created an eery sound against the rocks we were beginning to climb. We wore no shoes or sandals, of course, and the rocks were cold and sometimes sharp.

Suddenly I realized that we were not walking toward the admiral's quarters. In fact, we had passed through the gate of the fort and were walking and climbing over rocks leading toward the northeastern tip of the island.

"Courage, André!" Verneuil again whispered.

It was at that moment that intense fear gripped my being. I had been so naive that I had not appreciated what we were up against. I knew we risked much by writing our confession but I had honestly thought that all that could happen to us might be imprisonment for a few weeks, at the worst, or, as had happened with many others with whom Villegaignon disagreed, exile.

"Are we to be killed?" I asked.

"There is that possibility," Bourdel said cryptically.

"That is the actuality!" Matthieu Verneuil declared. "Why else would we be marching in this place, outside the fort, so early in the morning, before the colony is awake?"

"Silence!" shouted Gardien.

"But there was no trial!" I whispered.

"We had our trial last night," said Bourdel.

"You are to be silent!" Gardien again commanded.

But instead of being silent, Bourdel began to sing. It was a hymn we knew well and had sung often, a paraphrase of Psalm 100. Its tune was written by Louis Bourgeois, the choirmaster in Geneva. We sang it as we marched, with a crescendo of triumph, to the amazement of Gardien and the Scottish Guards.

150

All people that on earth do dwell,
Sing to the Lord with cheerful voice,
Him serve with mirth,
His praise forth tell,
Come ye before Him and rejoice!

"Him serve with mirth!" What a strange and significant line,
I thought, *in this, our tragic situation.* But the singing already
made me feel better.

O enter then His gates with praise,
Approach with joy His courts unto;
Praise, laud, and bless His name always,
For it is seemly so to do.

We were now quite close to Villegaignon and La Faucille,
who were standing and awaiting us. I knew they could hear us
but they said nothing as we continued to sing.

For why? The Lord our God is good,
His mercy is forever sure;
His truth at all times firmly stood,
And shall from age to age endure!

Not until that moment did I fully appreciate something I
had already taken for granted—that singing, that praise to
God in all circumstances, was integral and basic in the faith of
my Calvinist brothers. We were so often accused of being
sombre and humorless, as if Frenchmen could ever be that!
We were a singing people of faith.

We now stood before the admiral.

"Jean du Bourdel!" commanded Villegaignon in a gruff
and stern voice as Jean stepped forward. "Do you continue to
support what you have written and signed?"

"I do, governor," said Bourdel. "And I will continue to do
so until I am convinced by the authority of Scripture that I
have been in error."

"The time for argument has passed," said the admiral.

"Make your preparations!"

And now we clearly saw what the Scottish guards had been carrying.

First, they attached extra weights to Bourdel's shackled feet. These were cannonshot, to which extra links of chain had been affixed. I looked at Gardien who avoided my gaze. These were items he had made in his smithy shop.

"Excellency, may I be permitted to offer a prayer?" asked Bourdel.

"Pray!" Villegaignon made it sound as though he were commanding rather than granting a man's last wish.

"Forgive us our debts, O Father," Bourdel prayed, "as I shall try to forgive my debtors." He opened his eyes and looked at Villegaignon, Faucille, and Gardien. "Father, I do forgive them for they know not what they do!" And again he closed his eyes, looking toward heaven. "Father, into thy hands I commend my spirit. Amen."

Bourdel then turned to Matthieu and me. "My brothers," he smiled without a trace of fear, "be steadfast and immovable, always abounding in the work of the Lord, knowing that, in the Lord, your labor is not in vain."

I recognized it as a quotation from Paul's letter to the Corinthian Christians.

"Proceed!" shouted Villegaignon.

The guards then produced a sack made from some homespun cloth. With a shock, I realized that this was something I myself had sewn. I had been asked one day to make twenty-five of these. I thought that perhaps they would be used to store grain. Again I looked at Gardien and for a quick moment our eyes met. I thought to myself, *let us pity each other, Gardien; you made your instrument of death and I, too, have shared in this miserable business.*

A shudder climbed my spine as I saw the sack placed over Bourdel's head, and then tied tightly around his waist. His hands were shackled so that he could not untie the rope around his waist.

"To the rock!" the admiral commanded. "And Gardien, if you don't work faster, I'll have you whipped! There is too much delay!"

"Here, Bourdel," Gardien said softly, "it will be easier if you carry these weights." The cannonballs were heavy and Gardien lifted them with difficulty and placed them in Bourdel's shackled hands. I rushed forward to help him.

"Stand back, La Fon!" the governor warned me.

Gardien took Bourdel by an elbow and guided him up the few remaining steps to the top of the boulder, known on this island as The Rock.

"Gardien, now!" shouted Villegaignon in a fury.

Gardien quickly whispered something which the rest of us could not hear. He then gave Bourdel a quick but firm shove and Bourdel fell into the water.

We heard the splash but we were standing below the high rock and did not see where he fell. Besides, in my case, I had closed my eyes, breathing a prayer to God to be especially good to this man who had been so faithful to Him.

The water was known to be quite deep at this spot, perhaps seven or eight fathoms. Bourdel was shackled and could not move. The extra forty pounds or more of weight would carry him downward quickly. Surely death would come quickly as well, either by drowning or suffocation or both. And soon Matthieu and I would know just how fast or how slowly death would come.

The admiral again shouted. "Matthieu Verneuil! Come forward!"

The executions were not to be delayed. The governor was anxious to get on with the job. Perhaps he himself was afraid of what the other colonists would do if they knew that this horror was taking place.

"Verneuil, do you support what was written and what you have signed?" Villegaignon asked.

"I do," Matthieu replied.

The admiral placed a hand upon Verneuil's shoulder.

"Verneuil, I bear no hatred toward you," he said. "I know that you did not write this confession."

"I did sign it, governor. Willingly."

"Yes, but the instigator of this treason is now dead. Should we not leave the matter there? Do you wish, truly, also to die?"

"Monsieur Villegaignon, let me ask you this. Have we ever robbed you or injured you in any way? Have we ever conspired against your life?"

"There is the matter of your spying."

"We are not spies, admiral, and I believe you know it. I ask you again, have we committed any crimes against you or against this colony?"

"You have come to the rock for other reasons, Matthieu Verneuil. You are here because you are separated from the one true church, because rotten branches must be cut off so that the rest of the colony will not suffer corruption."

I now realized that we were victims of a new inquisition by a self-appointed inquisitor, a French Torquemada. Our governor was mad.

"Is there any alternative, sire?" asked Verneuil.

"What do you mean?"

"Instead of death, would you consider making me a prisoner for life, or even your slave?" I was quite surprised at what Matthieu had asked.

"Ah, you waver!" exclaimed the admiral. "That is good! If you would only retract your confession, I would most certainly consider alternatives. Yes!"

"I spoke only to test you, monsieur. I much prefer to live with my Lord in Heaven."

And Matthieu began to pray. "Eternal God, we die today for Your cause, for the cause of Your Son Jesus Christ, and for the defense of Your Holy Word and doctrine. Remember Your servants and help them! It is Your cause, and neither the devil nor any power in this world can ever gain the victory!"

Villegaignon turned away from Verneuil. He did not watch as Gardien and the guards repeated the process of shackles, weights, and mask.

As Matthieu was pushed into the chill water I heard his cry, "Lord Jesus, have mercy upon me!"

Christe eleison.

And now it would be my opportunity to face the challenge. I prayed for strength and endurance.

As I opened my eyes, I saw that a group of marines was approaching us. They were talking and joking loudly and they were carrying Pierre Bourdon on a litter.

The admiral had not forgotten Pierre.

"Be quiet!" he said to the marines. "The colony will be awake soon enough."

"We told this one we were bringing him to the island for the treatment he needed," said Raoul, the huge ruffian who had taken us into custody only yesterday. "We didn't tell him what kind of treatment," he laughed.

"Enough!" commanded Villegaignon. "Set him down. Pierre Bourdon, I ask you the same question I have asked the others. Do you continue to support what has been written in the confession and which you signed?"

So poor Pierre was to be the next victim.

"We have all been condemned?" Pierre asked weakly.

"Yes."

He looked about and saw me. "Two of my companions have already been killed?" It was painful for him to speak.

"Yes."

"Am I to be condemned without a trial, monsieur? I was not here when the others were brought to the island yesterday."

"I have asked if you continue to support the confession you signed."

"André," he called to me, "is he talking about the confession we signed, or did he make changes in it?"

"It is the same confession we signed," I said, huskily.

"Then I support it, monsieur."

"And then you are condemned because you signed a scandalous and a heretical statement which we consider to be treasonous."

"That is the sentence?"

"That is my judgment."

"Monsieur, you owe it to me to tell me at which point the confession I signed is heretical." Pierre was now sitting up and speaking in a much stronger voice. I did not know he had such strength left in his being. "For the good of my own soul, monsieur!" He was close to shouting. "Every man deserves to know why he is being put to death. I do not consider myself a heretic but if God has given you some special revelation, then show me my errors so I may be spared the horrors of hell!"

"There isn't enough time to convince any stubborn Huguenot of the error of his ways!" shouted the admiral.

"You could not prove anything from Scripture, monsieur. Not anything!"

"Gardien! Proceed!"

The admiral would not be stopped in his hurry to end whatever threat he felt we presented to his person.

Pierre Bourdon also prayed, in a firm voice. Gardien had lifted him from the pallet and was holding him so he would not fall.

"Lord God in heaven, may I with my companions fight Your good fight with honor and glory. Grant me Your grace. O Lord, pardon my sins. Be merciful to my dear wife." His voice broke momentarily. "And to my son," he whispered. "I pray in the name of Your most loving Son, my Lord and Saviour, Jesus Christ!"

Please God, I prayed, *may he have his son, a son who will be worthy of such a father.*

And the ritual of affixing shroud and shackles was again repeated.

There was a third splash of water and Pierre would shortly find himself in a new kingdom.

"And now we come to you, André La Fon," Villegaignon said as he beckoned to me.

"May I be forgiven if I have offended anyone." I said this to both Villegaignon and to Gardien. But I looked steadfastly at Gardien who had once been my friend and who did not relish the task before him.

"Forgiveness is neither simple nor easy," said the admiral. "I truly regret that you have come to this place, La Fon. You are the last and the others will not know if you now reject the confession you signed."

I did not answer.

"I cannot show partiality, La Fon. I cannot easily forgive, but I can pardon," he continued. "Gardien, you are his friend. Talk to him!"

Gardien led me some distance away so that the guards and the marines would not hear us.

"I think he wants to save your life, André!" Gardien said.

"Why?" I asked. "Why am I different? Why should I be treated differently?"

"Perhaps it is because you are an old man. Perhaps because you are a good tailor."

"Those are not sufficient reasons."

"Look, you can say you are not versed in the Holy Scriptures, no?"

"He wants me to retract, to renege. I believe in what was written."

"At least you could say you don't wish to remain inflexible. That was a term the admiral used when he spoke to me about this."

"What is that supposed to mean?"

"That you have an open mind. You are willing to be convinced of your error."

"I can't reject the thing for which my friends died!"

"But it was Bourdel's document. He wrote it, not you! You can't claim to be as educated as he. You are a tailor, he was a schoolmaster. Surely you could admit that you might be in error, that you honestly did not understand everything that you signed!"

"It's no use," I said. "I can't do it."

"André," Gardien said as he placed a hand on mine, "three men have already died. I shall remember this damnable day as long as I shall live. I don't want to kill you, of all people. I don't need a fourth death on my conscience!"

I shook my head and we returned to where the admiral and his troops were standing.

"Well?" Villegaignon asked. "Shall there be a pardon?"

"Excellency," I began, "it is not the pardon of men which is important but the pardon of God."

"Agreed," he said. "But we are speaking about men and laws of men. Do you support the confession?"

"It bears my signature."

"Do you support the confession, every article in it? Every argument, every answer?"

He was trying, desperately, to provide me with a way of escape. My heart was beating rapidly. I could hear the splashing of waves against the nearby rocks and each splash brought each of my companions clearly to mind. I suddenly remembered how I had always detested water and that I had never learned to swim. My fear was returning. I tried to remember the words of the hymn we had sung which had taken away my fear, but I found myself shaking.

"You must give me an answer, La Fon!" Villegaignon insisted.

I silently asked God to help me and in a flash I remem-

158

bered the words Jean Bourdel had used to answer the admiral, only a few minutes before. They seemed to me to be the answer to my prayer, the words I should speak!

"Excellency," I said, "I have never wished to be impertinent nor obstinate. I will retract the confession whenever its errors are proved to me by the Word of God, by Holy Scripture!"

I sighed, deeply. I had come so very close to defeat, to giving in to my fear, to a retraction of what I believed. But I had kept the faith! I took the stand Bourdel had taken. Unless errors could be proved by Scripture, I would not admit to errors.

"Excellent, La Fon!" The admiral was beaming. I could not believe my eyes or ears. "You made a very clever and a very good response. I congratulate you."

I wondered if, for a moment, I had taken leave of my senses.

"Remove his irons!"

It was not possible, I had retracted nothing!

"Soon we shall have the report from the scholars at the Sorbonne," said the admiral. "When it comes, it will be quite simple to prove the errors of your confession from Holy Scripture. Until that day, you are a free man!"

17. La Fon

The admiral had said I would be a free man.

A free man?

I sit in my cell with pen in hand, writing down my memories on paper which Gardien smuggles in to me.

The scholars from the Sorbonne have yet to send their reply.

And so I am free to be a tailor to the admiral and to his officers. And freely each day I return to my cell, which is now my home. I am free to be guarded at every step. I am free to be given food and a place to live, but no money for my labors. I am free to dream that some day I may be able to leave this place. I am free to be a prisoner for the rest of my life.

The island is less busy than it once was. Many people have left, some to Olaria on the mainland, others who have returned to France. Most of the colonists have gone. Those who remain are soldiers or marines, those who are loyal to Villegaignon and who were not shocked by the massacre of the three Huguenots.

I am told that our defenses are only a facade, that should we be attacked by the Portuguese, we should doubtless be defeated.

I have a window in my cell and it faces the water. I go to sleep each night hearing the lapping of the waves, the washing of water against rocks and sand. I hope some day that the water will wash away the memories of the faces and sounds of my friends who await the resurrection.

In my own mind, I did not renounce my beliefs. I thought I had repeated what Bourdel had said. I now know that I said more than Bourdel had said, and I said it poorly. It is still my conviction that unless I am convinced by God's Word of my error, I will renounce nothing. The admiral heard what he wanted to hear, he twisted what he heard, and made it appear that I had retreated from the affirmations of our confession.

Gardien knows better. We have spoken many times, many nights, about that confession and what the Scriptures teach regarding true discipleship. Villegaignon would be aghast to know how much of the Reformed faith his chief jailer and executioner has already adopted as his own.

But the people who live here and in Olaria believe me to be a renegade, an opportunist, a man whose spirit and will was broken and who retracted his confession. I have heard that Jean de Lery also believes this. This saddens me greatly.

Why this should have happened to me, I do not understand. I was the oldest of our group. I had lived my life. I now wish with all of my being that I had been able to offer my life in sacrifice with those of my brothers.

"Be thou faithful unto death!" says the Scripture.

There are many who believe that I was unfaithful.

And as I hear the stormy lashing of the waves, as I do this night, there are moments when I would agree with them.

However, I intend still to be faithful unto death. I, too, have been sentenced and my death is slower and much more painful.

I was once shown the motto and coat of arms of John Calvin. It shows a flaming heart upon an opened, outstretched hand, and it declares: "My heart I give Thee, Lord, eagerly and entirely."

And I do, too.

Epilogue

Pastor Richier and his companions on the caravelle *Jacques* did reach France. Richier was arrested but soon released after Villegaignon's letters were read. The Sorbonne scholars apparently did not choose to answer the admiral's questions.

Jean de Lery also returned to France, taking with him his notes and journals, and a copy of the martyrs' confession. He shared his notes with Jean Crespin who, in 1564, the year John Calvin died, first told this story in a book titled *About The Church of the Faithful in the Country of Brazil.*

Pastor Richier and Admiral Villegaignon both wrote memoirs. The admiral died in France, prior to 1564, of some sort of incurable disease, according to Crespin, and in disgrace.

Admiral Coligny, for whom the colony was named, finally declared himself to be a Huguenot, in 1559. He became the first victim of the Saint Bartholomew's Massacre in 1572.

The small colony at Coligny was overrun by the Portuguese, under Mem de Sá, in 1567.

We know nothing about the fate of André La Fon.

However, there is some curious speculation regarding Jacques de Balleur, the Huguenot who chose to escape. A public hanging was reported in 1567, the year Coligny fell, in a small village named Rio de Janeiro. A heretic was hanged by the Portuguese priest, José de Anchieta. We have the name of the heretic who was hanged—the name, Boles. There are many Presbyterians in Brazil, who continue the Calvinistic heritage, who firmly believe that "Boles" was "Balleur."

The former island of Coligny is today called Villegaignon. The island is adjacent to the Metropolitan Airport of Santos Dumont, in Rio, and every passenger who looks for it will see it.

The Martyrs' Confession

The Martyrs' Confession first appeared in Jean Crespin's book. Domingos Ribeiro translated it into Portuguese in a version which appeared in Rio de Janeiro in 1917, from which the following translation has been made. Admiral Villegaignon's questions have been reconstructed and inserted within the Confession; the questions do not appear in the published version. This statement of faith, written entirely by laymen, was the first Confession to be formulated in the Americas.

The Confession

According to the doctrine of Saint Peter, the apostle, as recorded in his first epistle, all Christians must always be ready to give a reason for the hope that is within them, and to do this with gentleness and kindness. Thus, we who have signed this document with one accord, according to the measure of grace which the Lord has granted to us, do give our reason for the hope within us to Monsieur Villegaignon, point by point, as he has requested.

1. Do you accept the Trinity?

We believe in one God, immortal and invisible, creator of heaven and earth, creator of all things visible and invisible, who is distinct in three persons: the Father, the Son, and the Holy Spirit; who, nevertheless, are of one substance, in an eternal essence; who are also of one will. We believe in the Father, the fountain and beginning of all good; in the Son, eternally generated by the Father, who, in the fullness of time, made Himself known to the world in the flesh, conceived by the Holy Spirit, born of the Virgin Mary, made under the law to rescue those who lived under the law, so that we might be adopted as proper sons ourselves; and we believe in the Holy Spirit, proceeding from the Father and the Son, teacher of all truth, who spoke through the mouths of the prophets, and who inspired all things said by our Lord Jesus Christ and the Apostles. The Holy Spirit is our comforter in affliction, who keeps us steadfast, and helps us to persevere in all that is good.

In our individual lives we believe it is necessary only to worship and perfectly love our God, invoking His majesty through faith.

2. Do you distinguish the natures of Jesus Christ?

Since we worship one Lord Jesus Christ, we do not separate one nature from another, believing that His two natures, the divine and the human, are inseparable in Him.

3. What do you believe regarding the Holy Spirit?

Regarding the Son of God and the Holy Spirit, we believe that which God's Word, apostolic doctrine, and the symbols teach us.

4. Do you accept a final judgment?

We believe that our Lord Jesus Christ will come to judge the living and the dead and that He will return in a visible and human form, just as He ascended into heaven; that He will carry out that judgment in the manner predicted in Saint Matthew 25; He will have complete power to judge, albeit in the form of a man, through the power given Him by the Father.

In our prayers, we say that the Father will appear at the end time in the person of the Son. We understand this to mean that the power of the Father will be demonstrated in that judgment; we do not intend to confuse between these persons, inasmuch as They are distinct one from the other.

5. What is your understanding of the Blessed Sacrament?

We believe that in the Most Holy Sacrament of the Last Supper, through the material elements of bread and wine, faithful souls are actually and truly fed with the substance of our Lord Jesus Christ, just as our bodies are fed with food. We are not saying by this that the bread and the wine are transformed or transubstantiated into His body and blood, because the bread continues in its nature and substance to be bread, just as the wine remains wine, without change or alteration.

However, we distinguish between this particular bread and wine and other bread which is dedicated to common use, since, for us, these are sacramental symbols through which truth is infallibly received.

This does not occur except through faith. It is not something we prepare nor can we prepare ourselves for it. As Saint Augustine says, "Why do you prepare your teeth and belly? Believe, and you will eat it!"

Thus, the symbol itself does not give us some special truth or significant thing; rather, it is our Lord Jesus Christ, through His power, virtue, and goodness, who sustains and preserves our souls, making them to be participants in His body, His blood, and in all of His benefits.

Let us look at the words of Jesus Christ, "This bread is my body."

Tertullian, writing in his fourth book against Marcion, explains those words in this fashion: "This is the symbol and sign of my body."

Saint Augustine says, "The Lord did not avoid saying 'This is my body' when he gave only the symbol of his body."

As was ordered in the first Canon of the Council of Nicea, in this holy sacrament we must not imagine anything carnal, we must not be distracted from the bread and the wine, because these are the symbols to lift our spirits to heaven, so that by faith we may see the Son of God, our Lord Jesus Christ, sitting at the right hand of God, His Father.

In this respect, we could add certain references of Saint Augustine to the Ascension, but we omit these, fearing that they may be too extensive.

6. Why do you not mix water with the sacramental wine?

We believe that if it were necessary to add water to the wine, the writers of the Gospels and Saint Paul himself would not have omitted telling us something of such great importance.

As for the early church Fathers who may have observed this custom, we cannot agree that it is essential today. They may have based their observance on the fact that blood mixed with water flowed from the side of Jesus Christ at His crucifixion, an event which occurred after the institution of the Holy Supper; we believe its observance must be based upon God's Word.

7. What occurs at the consecration of the elements?

We believe there is no consecration other than that made by a minister when he commemorates the supper, that he repeats the actual institution of this Supper, in the form prescribed by our Lord Jesus Christ, in a language understood by the people, which reminds them of the death and passion of our Lord. As Saint Augustine puts it, it is both a consecration and a word of faith, preached and received in faith. Thus, secret or mystical words spoken over the elements do not appear in the institution left to the Apostles by our Lord Jesus Christ, who gave His words directly to the disciples who were present at the Supper, commanding them to eat and to drink.

8. Is not the Holy Sacrament a food?

The Holy Sacrament of the Supper is not a food for the body but a food for souls (as we have already declared in proposition 5), not something material, and which is received only by faith.

9. How do you understand Baptism?

We believe that baptism is a sacrament of penitence, that it is an entrance to the Church of God, whereby we are incorporated into Jesus Christ. Baptism for us symbolizes a forgiveness of past and future sins, achieved clearly and only through the death of our Lord Jesus.

Moreover, the overcoming (the mortification) of our flesh is symbolized by the washing, shown to us by the water poured upon the child, which is a sign and seal of the blood of our Lord Jesus, who alone purifies our souls.

This institution is taught to us in the Word of God and was observed by the holy Apostles, who used water in the name of the Father, the Son, and the Holy Spirit. As for exorcisms, the renouncing of Satan, the use of oil, spittle, and salt, we believe these to be human traditions; and we are content with the form of the sacrament left to us by our Lord Jesus.

10. Do you believe in free will?

We believe that if the first man, created in the image of God, had full liberty and will, equally to do good or evil, then only he fully understood the nature of free will within that integrity. Since he did not retain this gift of God, it was taken from him because of his sin, and from all his descendents. Thus no son of Adam, of himself, is good.

This is why Saint Paul says that the sensual man does not understand the things of God. Hosea exclaims to the children of Israel:

170

"Your perdition is of yourselves, O Israel!" This is the condition of the man who is not regenerated by the Holy Spirit.

As for the man who is a Christian, baptized in the blood of Jesus Christ, walking in newness of life, our Lord Jesus Christ restores in him a free will, a will that has been reformed for good works. This does not necessarily mean perfection because doing good is not ultimately in his power, but this comes from God. The Holy Apostle declares in the seventh chapter of his letter to the Romans that "that which I would, I cannot do."

The person who is predestined to eternal life, even though he sins by virtue of the weakness of being human, nevertheless that person cannot fall into a permanent state of stubborn refusal to repent.

This is why Saint John says that he does not sin because his election remains within him.

11. Do you believe in the forgiveness of sins, in absolution?

We believe that forgiveness of sins belongs only to the Word of God, of which, according to Saint Ambrose, man is only its minister. If the minister condemns or absolves, it is not he who does this, but the Word of God which he proclaims.

In this regard, Saint Augustine says that it is not through men's merit that sins are forgiven but, rather, through the power of the Holy Spirit. The Lord commanded his apostles, "Receive the Holy Spirit;" later He added, "If you forgive someone his sins, they shall be forgiven."

12. Should the clergy not be ordained by the laying on of hands?

This custom served in its time but there is no need to conserve it now. It is not possible to give someone the Holy Spirit through such laying on of hands. That gift pertains only to God.

13. Do you believe in divorce?

The separation of a man and a woman who were legitimately

united in marriage may not occur except in the case of adultery, as our Lord taught. See Saint Matthew 19:5.* Not only may separation take place for this cause, but after the magistrate has investigated the matter, and if the innocent party cannot curb his or her passion, then that party may remarry, as Saint Ambrose says in his commentary on chapter 7 of the First Epistle to the Corinthians. The magistrate, however, must proceed in this matter with mature counsel.

14. Should bishops marry?

Saint Paul, teaching that a bishop should be the husband of one wife, does not insist that the bishop should be married. Rather, the apostle condemns bigamy, which was something that afflicted mankind in those times. However, we leave this question to the judgment of those who are more knowledgeable in the Scriptures. Our faith does not stand or fall on this point.

15. Should the clergy marry?

We should render only those vows to God of which He approves. Thus, monastic vows tend only to corrupt the true service of God. It is rash and presumptuous for a man to assume vows which go beyond his vocation, especially in view that the Scriptures teach us that continence is a special gift. See Saint Matthew 15 and 1 Corinthians 7. It follows that those who renounce marriage for life cannot be excused of grave rashness and excessive confidence in themselves.

In this way they tempt God, since the gift of continence for some is only temporary, and he who has it for a time may not have it for his entire life. Thus, monks, priests, and others who obligate themselves and promise to live in chastity, tempt God because it is not within themselves to fulfill what they have promised.

Saint Cyprian, in chapter 11, says: "If the virgins dedicate themselves in good will to Christ, they persevere in chastity without fault; if they are thus strong and constant, they await the reward prepared for their virginity; if they do not care for nor cannot

*This is the reference that was cited. Verse 9 may have been meant.

persevere in their vows, it is better that they marry rather than fall into the flames of lasciviousness."

As for the passage of Saint Paul which refers to widows, it is true that widows, chosen to serve the Church, should agree not to remarry, for as long as they do this work. This does not grant them some kind of sanctity; it is simply that they could not carry out their assignments well if they were married. Further, if they wish to marry, the teaching is that they should renounce the vocation to which God called them, in order not to violate the promise made at baptism, namely that "everyone should serve God in the vocation to which he was called." Widows, then, do not take a vow of continence ... Moreover, to avoid just such a situation, the Apostle Saint Paul, in the chapter already referred to, prescribes that such persons not assume such vows unless they are at least sixty years of age, an age, generally speaking, beyond incontinence.

16. Do you believe in the Saints?

We believe that Jesus Christ is our only Mediator, intercessor, and advocate, through whom we have access to the Father, and, justified through His blood, we shall be free of death, and since we are already reconciled through Him, we shall be victorious over death.

As for the saints who have died, we believe they wish for our salvation, the fulfillment of God's kingdom, and that the number of the elect be completed. However, we need not direct petitions to them as intercessors, for in this we would disobey God's commandment. We who are alive, who are united as members of one body, we must pray one for the other, as so many passages of Holy Scripture teach us.

17. Do you pray for the dead?

As for those who have died, Saint Paul, in 1 Thessalonians 4, prohibits us from sorrowing for them, in the manner of pagans who have no hope of the resurrection. The apostle does not urge us nor teach us to pray for the dead—and he would not have forgotten this if this were proper. Psalm 48* declares that the spirits of the dead

*Psalm 49.

receive what they earned during their lifetime; thus if they accomplished nothing while they were alive, they receive nothing additional when they are dead.

This is the answer we give to the propositions you sent to us, according to the measure of faith God has granted to us, to whom we pray that our faith not die until it produce fruits worthy of God's sons. Thus, as we grow and persevere in that faith we give thanks and praise to Him forever. Amen. Thus may it be!

Jean du Bourdel
Matthieu Verneuil
Pierre Bourdon
André La Fon